TIGER ADVENTURE

The shopkeeper told them. 'Look out for the Yeti. They are very bad this year.'

'What are the Yeti?' Hal asked.

'Your people call them the Abominable Snowmen. Our own name for them is Yeti.'

'That's a better name for them,' Hal said. 'very short and easy to say. Yeti.'

Roger added, 'That was one thing Dad wanted us to do – investigate the Abominable Snowman.'

The shopkeeper said, 'Many people who go up never come down again. They are killed by the Yeti. The Yeti eat them. We never find their bodies or their bones.'

'What is a Yeti?' Hal asked. 'A man or a beast?'

'No one knows. We don't know what they are like. They are invisible. If you see a Yeti, you die. Some say they are ten feet tall. Others say a Yeti is a monster ninety feet tall and forty feet through.'

'But do you have any proof that these monsters exist?' Hal asked.

'One was here last night,' said the shopkeeper. 'Come outside and I'll show you his footprints.'

by the same author

ARCTIC ADVENTURE
AMAZON ADVENTURE
SOUTH SEA ADVENTURE
UNDERWATER ADVENTURE
VOLCANO ADVENTURE
WHALE ADVENTURE
AFRICAN ADVENTURE
ELEPHANT ADVENTURE
SAFARI ADVENTURE
LION ADVENTURE
GORILLA ADVENTURE
DIVING ADVENTURE
CANNIBAL ADVENTURE

TIGER
ADVENTURE

by

WILLARD PRICE

Illustrated by

PAT MARRIOTT

RED FOX

A Red Fox Book

Published by Random House Children's Books
61-63 Uxbridge Road, London W5 5SA

A division of Random House UK Ltd
London Melbourne Sydney Auckland
Johannesburg and agencies throughout the world

First published in 1979 by Jonathan Cape Ltd
Paperback edition 1980 Knights Books

Red Fox edition 1993

10

Set in 11/12.5pt Baskerville by Intype, London
Printed and bound in Great Britain by
Cox & Wyman Ltd, Reading, Berkshire

Addresses for companies within The Random House Group Limited
can be found at:
www.randomhouse.co.uk/offices.htm

RANDOM HOUSE UK Limited Reg. No. 954009
www.kidsatrandomhouse.co.uk

ISBN 9780099184911

The Random House Group Limited supports The Forest Stewardship
Council (FSC), the leading international forest certification organisation.
All our titles that are printed on Greenpeace approved FSC certified paper
carry the FSC logo. Our paper procurement policy can be found at:
www.rbooks.co.uk/environment.

Contents

1	Surprise	7
2	The World's Wildest Animal	12
3	Tiny Tim and the Giant	19
4	Three Prizes	27
5	The Laughing Leopard	34
6	The Playful Panda	43
7	Runaway Elephant	49
8	The Great Round-up	55
9	The Boy and the Beast	64
10	The Crazy-Cat Who Eats Himself	69
11	Friends or Enemies?	74
12	Another 'King of Beasts'	80
13	Lion Lost	88
14	Roger's Tiger	97
15	Roger Goes to Jail	106
16	A Camel Named Jeremiah	114
17	Troubles of a Wild Boar	122
18	Midnight Monster	128
19	Wolf and Dogwolf	137
20	The Houseboat	143
21	Roger's Wild Buffalo	153
22	Saved by a Monkey	161
23	Hal's Sloth Bear	166

24 Up, Up, Up   171
25 Bats for Breakfast   181
26 Hunting the Horrible Yeti   190
27 The Deadly Avalanche   201
28 The Snow Leopard   208
29 The White Tiger   217
30 The Yeti Mystery   223
31 Mountains Make Men   230
32 What's a Father For?   235

1
Surprise

Roger stared at the tiger. The tiger stared at Roger.

The tiger had just come out of the woods. It was so astonished to meet a human that it stood rooted to the spot. Roger was also rooted.

What an enormous animal! Roger had never before seen a cat of this size. Back in Africa, he had seen many lions and thought they were the kings of the cat world. But this huge beast seemed twice as large. Fourteen-year-old Roger was a big boy weighing one hundred and thirty pounds — this animal must weigh more than twice that.

What to do? He had no gun. He and his brother Hal, nineteen, and bigger than most men, were not in India to shoot wild animals — but to take them alive. But how could a boy take this monster alive?

It was more likely that the beast, standing there like a statue, would take Roger alive.

Roger had learned enough about wild animals to know that if he turned and ran, the great beast would be after him in a flash.

He had lived with wild animals all of his fourteen years. His father, John Hunt, had an animal farm on Long Island near New York. There he kept all sorts of wild creatures. John Hunt was an animal collector from whom the zoos could buy almost any creature they wanted, from elephant to mouse. He stayed in Long Island, while his two sons roamed abroad to find the game he needed. Hunt's latest cable had read:

TIGERS. GREATEST OF THE WORLD'S CATS. CAREFUL. DON'T GET MAULED. BEST PLACE TO FIND THEM — INDIA, THE HIMALAYAS. ALSO WE COULD USE SNOW LEOPARD, HIMALAYAN BEAR, INDIAN ELEPHANT, RHINO, WILD BOAR, PANDA, SLOTH BEAR, GIR LION, WOLF, HYENA, SAMBAR, GAUR, WILD BUFFALO, HOODED COBRA. INVESTIGATE ABOMINABLE SNOWMAN. YOU'VE DONE FAMOUSLY. LOVE FROM YOUR MOTHER AND ME. JOHN HUNT.

And now — here was one of the animals their father wanted most, the tiger. Roger stood within ten feet of this prize, and could do nothing.

Suddenly he heard a pop. A dart whistled through the air and its point pierced the tiger's flank. It carried a medicine that would go into the tiger's arteries and make him go to sleep. Good old Hal — he had been on the job after all.

But the tiger hadn't seen Hal. He thought the prick in his side was made by the boy in front of him. With a mighty roar he leaped towards Roger who at once took to his heels. Would the beast go to sleep before Roger became its breakfast?

Ha! A river! Roger rushed to the bank and dived

in. He swam towards the other shore. He would fool this beast. He knew that most members of the cat family didn't swim. The lions in Africa never swam. The tiger was a cat, and therefore couldn't swim. Roger could almost laugh. After all, he had been pretty clever to think of this way of escape.

But what was that splashing behind him? He glanced back. He suddenly learned something about tigers. Tigers *love* water. They are expert swimmers. So expert that this tiger was gaining on him fast. A second more and it would grab him, force him under water, drown him, then drag him ashore and eat him.

He clambered up on the shore. A reception committee was waiting for him. Another tiger! Perhaps the mate of the first. Two tigers! That was just two tigers too many.

He slipped around the first tiger which had just come out of the river, shaking itself like a dog and showering him with water. Roger promptly dived in and swam back to the shore he had just left.

Hal stood on the bank. Also, four tiger cubs. And it occurred to Roger that the tiger who had faced him was not exactly a tiger, but a tigress, the mother of these cubs. So that was why the tigress had refused to run from him — she was defending her cubs, unseen in the bushes. Now the cubs were mewing anxiously as their mother chased Roger back where he had come from.

Hal pulled his brother out on to the bank. The tiger did not follow. Why? Because the sleep drug had taken effect. The beast gave up just short of

the bank. Her head sank into the water. The cubs whined. In a moment their mother would drown.

Together, the boys pulled up the heavy head and rested it on the bank so that the animal, although asleep, could still breathe. The cubs at once crowded round, licking the river water from their mother's face.

Father John Hunt wanted a tiger. Here was a beauty.

'The truck,' said Roger. 'Bring back the truck.'

But Hal did not move.

'No,' he said. 'This is not our tiger. Her cubs need her.'

'Take the cubs too,' Roger suggested.

'Too young,' Hal said. 'They would never stand the trip halfway round the world.'

Roger was disappointed. 'Never mind,' Hal said, 'we'll get our tiger yet. Let's go back a bit — I don't want to be here when Her Majesty wakes up.'

From a retreat in the bushes they watched until the tigress came to and, with her cubs, walked home in safety.

2
The World's Wildest Animal

One morning there was a knock on the door of the cabin where Hal and Roger lived.

Hal opened the door. A young man about his own age said, 'Are you Hal Hunt?'

'That's right.'

'My name is Vic Stone.'

'Come in. This is my brother, Roger.' Vic shook hands.

'Someone told me you fellows know a lot about animals. We're going for a ride tonight. Would you both like to come along?'

Hal looked at Roger. Roger nodded. 'Sure,' Hal said. 'It's a good time to see the animals. They come out on the road at night.'

'Fine,' said Vic, 'just what we want. We'll pick you up as soon as it gets dark.'

A Land-Rover — the big British car preferred by hunters — drove up after sunset. Vic had two companions, Jim and Harry. The five had plenty of room.

The Gir Forest wildlife sanctuary lies at the foot of the tallest mountains in the world — the Himalayas. The highest in the range is Mount Everest, twenty-nine thousand feet. These peaks were still bathed in sunshine, but the forest road had already become as dark as a tunnel. The car's lights were turned on and a powerful spotlight which could be pointed this way and that to pick out any beast in the road or on either side.

'Where are your rifles?' Vic asked.

'Rifles?' Hal was puzzled. 'I thought you knew. We never carry rifles.'

'Only knives?'

'No knives.'

Vic stopped the car. 'How do you expect to hunt without guns or knives? Don't you have anything?'

'Only this lasso.' Closely looped, it hung from Hal's shoulder. 'We don't kill animals. We take them alive.'

'Isn't that awfully dangerous?'

'So-so,' Hal said. 'I'd better explain. Our father is an animal collector. He sends us out to get the animals, then keeps them on his wild-animal farm until some zoo wants to buy a tiger, leopard, elephant or whatever.'

Vic started the car. The beam of the spotlight roamed back and forth.

'Look, a chital!' cried Roger. The chital was India's most beautiful deer. Both Jim and Harry shot at once. Jim misfired, Harry's bullet took off the left side of the chital's face and one eye, and smashed the skull. The injured beast leaped into the forest. Vic drove on.

13

'Wait a minute!' Hal shouted. 'Aren't you going to follow him up? You can't wound an animal terribly and leave him to suffer. You have to put him out of his misery — track him down and kill him.'

Vic laughed. 'What chance would we have of finding him in the woods?'

The next victim was a splendid Asiatic moose. It stood in the middle of the road staring at the lights of the oncoming car. It had an immense body supported on four rather slender legs. Its head was crowned by magnificent antlers.

Not knowing what was behind those lights, it charged the car at full speed. The crash did the car no harm but it ended the life of the moose. It slumped to the ground with a broken neck. Vic drove around it and went on. Hal felt sick.

The next to be wiped out was a langur monkey.

'You've killed your best friend,' Hal said. 'That's the monkey that gives you warning when any dangerous beast comes near. So you've not only killed your friend but you've made it likely that people who would have been warned by this monkey's voice will die.'

'Oh, cut the sermons, Hal. We're just out to have a good time. Don't louse it up. If you do we'll not take you again.'

'That's okay with me,' said Hal.

A wild water-buffalo loomed up ahead. What wonderful horns, eight feet across. Three shots rang out. The tough beast managed only to get to the side of the road before it lay down and died.

Then a splendid tiger.

'Stop here,' Hal said. 'I want this one.'

He started to get out of the car.

'You crazy idiot,' cried Vic. 'Stay in the car.'

'Don't shoot,' Hal said. 'No matter what he does.'

He took his lasso from his shoulder. He walked towards the tiger, still a hundred feet off. The tiger was staring into the light as if hypnotised. Hal kept on walking, very quietly, just outside the beam of the spotlight. The eyes of the beast were as green as traffic lights, but they did not mean 'Go'. Hal moved without sound, trying not to step on any crackling twigs. He shortened the distance to fifty feet, then forty, then thirty. The tiger caught sight of him and roared. That roar seemed to shake the whole forest. But it did not shake Hal's determination. He swung the lasso and let fly. It settled neatly over the tiger's head and rested on his neck. Hal pulled it tight. A knot in the rope prevented it from getting too tight and choking the animal.

Then came the fireworks. Roar on roar. The tiger's throat is ideally arranged for roaring. The tiger leaped, squirmed, threw his great weight about as he tried to snap the rope. It held fast because there was a core of steel in the centre of it. Then the tiger made a lunge, not towards Hal who was still in the shadows, but towards that greater enemy, the brightly lit car. Hal had already whipped the end of the rope round a tree and tied it fast. The line kept the tiger from reaching the car. Hal jumped in and away they went.

'I'll come back tomorrow and pick it up,' Hal said.

There were two other kills by the bloodthirsty playboys.

Then Hal noticed that a car was coming up on them from behind. It went in front of the Land-Rover and stopped, blocking the road. Two men got out and came up to the driver's side.

'Get over,' one said. 'I'll drive.'

'Who are you?' said Vic.

'Police.'

'What do you want?'

'Be patient. You'll find out.'

Two hours later they rolled into a small town and drew up in front of the police station. The two policemen ushered them inside and lined them up in front of the sergeant — then reported to the officer what these rascals had done.

'Boys,' said the sergeant, 'I hope you've had a good time — because you're not going to have another. You're going to have to pay a very heavy fine for what you have done. And you will be locked up until you pay it. You think you are the highest of the animals. You are the lowest. If the animals could tell you what they think of you I'm afraid the description would not be very complimentary. They would say that men like you are more dangerous than any of the so-called wild beasts. You are cruel and brutal and deserve what you are going to get.'

The three hoodlums were put in a cell but Hal and Roger held back.

'Come on,' said the sergeant. 'Get in there.'

'We don't belong with these fellows,' Hal said. 'We are doing just what you are doing, trying to preserve the wildlife. We did no shooting — you can see we have no guns. We are collecting some

16

of your wonderful animals to send back to our country so that our people can enjoy them.'

'But do you have any permit to do this?'

'Yes,' Hal said, drawing out a paper from his pocket. 'This is a permit signed by the Chief of Police in New Delhi.'

He handed it to the sergeant who looked at it critically, screwing up his forehead. Hal noticed that he was looking at it upside down.

'What language is this?' demanded the sergeant.

'It is in the two official languages of India — Hindi and English. You speak English very well, so you must be able to read it.'

'I can speak it,' said the sergeant, 'but I never went to school so I can't read it. I read only my own language. You understand of course that there are more than a thousand languages in India. You should have brought a permit in the language of the Gir country. I don't know whether this permit is good or not.'

'You can call up the Chief of Police in New Delhi and ask him. Give him our names — Hal Hunt and Roger Hunt.'

'No,' objected the sergeant. 'Don't you realise it is almost midnight? He won't be in his office. He will be at home sound asleep. I'm afraid you will just have to stay with us until morning.'

He turned to the police. 'Put these two in jail until morning. They are either very good men or very good liars. Don't put them with the rest of those skunks.'

So Hal and Roger had the luxury of a cell of their own. Cockroaches and fleas ran over them all

17

night. When morning came they still had to wait until almost noon when the Chief of Police arrived at his office. Then, with a good report, they were released and without breakfast or lunch, and covered with the bites of insects, they hired a truck and two men, stopped to load a very sleepy tiger, and transported it to one of the many cages they had installed near their cabin for the wild animals they expected to obtain in the Gir Forest.

Then to dinner — and the first one to be served was the tiger.

3
Tiny Tim and the Giant

Vic appeared. He and Hal stood watching the tiger enjoy his meal. It was certainly a fine animal.

'How much do you think she weighs?'

'It's a *he* this time,' Hal said. 'I guess that he'd tip the scales at five hundred pounds.'

'Hal,' Vic said, 'I want to apologise for last night. I don't know what got into me. I'm really not that kind of guy. That night in jail taught me a lesson that I'll never forget. The fine — that was terrible. Now I'm busted, flat broke.'

Roger came out of the cabin and was surprised to see Vic. He had hoped never to set eyes on him again.

'Flat broke,' Vic repeated. 'I was just wondering — I hate to ask — but I was thinking that you might lend me something. Just until I get a cheque from home. I'm expecting one any day now.'

Roger was shaking his head. He knew his brother. Hal was always willing to help. But surely he could see that this fellow was just trying to get something for nothing.

'How much do you need?' Hal said.

'Oh, just a little. Say two hundred dollars?'

Roger shook his head a little harder.

Hal took out his wallet. 'Rupees or dollars?'

'Make it dollars. I don't understand this rupee stuff.'

Hal shelled out two crisp hundred-dollar bills.

'Thanks a lot,' Vic said. 'I'll pay you back soon. The sergeant said good things about you. He made me see I was on the wrong track. Now I'd like to get on the right track. I thought perhaps I could help you get the animals you need.'

'Well, that's nice of you,' Hal said. 'This is a big job. I do need help. I'll pay you fifty dollars for every wild animal you bring in.'

Roger shook his head harder than ever. His neck was getting tired.

'Good,' said Vic. 'When do we start?'

'Right away,' Hal said. 'But this afternoon you'll have to work alone. Roger and I have to make this cage stronger if we want to keep the most powerful cat on earth. I see you have your rifle. Leave it in the cabin.'

'But I might need it. You know — in an emergency.'

'If you have a gun, you are likely to use it. Remember, the animal doesn't have a gun. Roger, take his gun and put it inside. I'll tell you what, Vic — I'll lend you my lasso.'

'That's too easy,' Vic protested. 'Anybody can throw a rope. But it takes a man to shoot a gun.'

'It's the other way round,' Hal said. 'Anybody can pull a trigger. But it takes a bit of skill to throw a lasso. And the difference is that the gun gives you a dead animal, and the lasso gives you a live one.'

Vic, after grumbling a little more, set out with the lasso over his shoulder.

Then Roger spoke up. With the wisdom of a fourteen-year-old he scolded his brother five years older. 'You dumb cluck! You'll never see that two hundred again. And as for fifty dollars for every wild animal, a caterpillar is a wild animal, and you'll have to pay him that if he brings one in.'

'Nonsense,' said Hal. 'You've got to have more faith in human nature. Anyhow, what else could we do? The fine cleaned him out. He had to have something to live on. I'm guessing that he's a city boy who has never had any experience in real hunting. He needs someone to teach him, and it seems that you and I will have to be the teachers.'

Hal was right. Vic was a city boy, and like every city boy he longed for adventure. His home was in Cleveland, Ohio, near Western Reserve-Case University. He was a college man if you can call a fellow who has spent only four months in college a college man. One term at university was enough for him. He preferred to roam around Wake Park Lake across the road from the college and to follow a stream through the woods up to the lovely lakes of Shaker Heights. But even this was not enough. He wanted to see the world. So, one night, he helped himself to his father's money with the excuse that it would have cost his father a lot of money to keep him in college, so why not take it and spend it on something even more educational — travel. He left

21

a note saying that if his father had the urge to give him more money it could be sent to him care of the American Embassy in New Delhi, capital of India.

Then he walked out, hitch-hiked his way to New York and stowed away in a lifeboat on a freighter bound for Calcutta. His Indian ramblings led him finally to the Gir Forest where he bought a rifle and fancied himself as a great hunter like Jim Corbett or Ernest Hemingway. And here he was, armed with nothing but a silly rope.

Vic, wandering through the forest, thinking about the meanness of Hal who gave him only two hundred dollars and offered only fifty dollars for every wild animal he brought in, nearly bumped into the largest and shyest deer in India. He didn't know it was the famous sambar that makes its home on the mountainside four thousand to fourteen thousand feet up, but comes down at times to enjoy the shade of the Gir Forest.

He saw that the animal had sharply pointed horns. The skin was a dark, smoky brown. The throat was covered with bristles and the tail was long.

Now, if he only had his gun. He tried to lasso but the animal was already moving away and the rope merely slapped him on the back and fell off.

Now a chital joined the sambar — Vic knew the chital because he had just killed one the night before. The two deer turned and looked defiantly at their tormentor. Deer stick together, help each other out.

The sambar was as big as a horse and the chital as big as a pony. Then Vic saw a third deer, but this one was smaller than a rabbit. He was to learn later that it was called a mouse-deer. Vic didn't know the correct name for it but he gave it a name, Tiny Tim.

Tiny Tim ran and got squarely between the chital and the sambar. The giant deer lowered its head and licked the hide of its little friend.

What an opportunity! Vic couldn't possibly miss all of them. He threw his lasso, hoping it would snare the antlers of the giant or the chital. He didn't care about Tiny Tim. It was too small to matter.

The lasso caught on the branch of a tree. At once a growl came from the same tree. Looking up, Vic saw a snarling leopard. It leaped to the ground and glared at Vic who decided that this was the last moment of his life. Luckily the sambar sounded. The leopard turned and made for the three deer. The sambar and chital ran. Tiny Tim was not so quick. The grass around him was as high as he was and prevented him from moving fast.

The sambar looked back at the little fellow struggling among the grass blades. The giant, risking death in the claws of the leopard, ran back, picked up Tiny Tim in his jaws and joined the chital in a race for safety.

The leopard, although the greatest killer in the cat world, could not keep up with the deer. They left him far behind and Vic heard him a mile away roaring his anger because his quarry had escaped him.

Vic went back to the Hunt cabin. He told the boys about his bravery in facing three deer and a leopard.

'Well, I don't suppose you got the leopard,' Hal said, 'but it's great that you brought home three deer. Did you put them in a cage?'

'No,' Vic admitted. 'I didn't bring back all three.'

'I suppose you got the two big ones.'

'Not exactly.'

'Too bad,' Hal said, 'but it's great that you got the mouse-deer. It can't go fast so it was easy to catch. It's really the most important of the three.

It's unique and valuable because of its remarkably small size. So we must congratulate you on bringing home one of the most unusual deer in the world. Where did you put it, this Tiny Tim as you call it?'

'I couldn't catch it.'

'But it's so easy to catch in the long grass and rocks. What was the trouble?'

'The big fellow came back and carried it off.'

Neither Hal nor Roger could think of anything more to say.

It was getting dark. Vic went to his quarters nearby. Roger was angry with Hal. He blamed Hal for taking on this stupid city bum.

As they entered the cabin Roger noticed something moving into a dark corner. It looked like a harmless garter snake. It was small, not more than four feet long.

'Good,' thought Roger. 'I'll give him a treat. I won't do anything but scare him half to death.'

After Hal was in bed and asleep, Roger picked up the snake by the tail and slipped it into Hal's bed. That suited the snake to a T. It snuggled up to Hal to get his warmth.

Hal woke, felt something squirming about on his ribs, let out a yell and threw the serpent out on the floor. Roger laughed till he ached.

'You love animals so much, how about that one?' he said.

Hal looked at the snake and his face went white.

'You don't need to worry,' Roger said. 'It's not poisonous.'

'Not poisonous!' roared Hal. 'That's a hooded cobra!'

Roger apologised. 'Gee whiz, I didn't know.' He fully expected Hal to blow up and was astonished when his patient brother merely dropped the snake into a burlap bag and said:

'That's just fine. One of the chief things we were told to get — a hooded cobra! Thanks a lot for what you did, little brother. And if you ever do it again I'll knock your head off.'

4
Three Prizes

Early in the morning Roger, Hal and Vic went back
to the spot where Vic had failed to capture the
sambar, chital and mouse-deer. Perhaps the animals
liked this place and would return to it.

The first thing Hal saw was a rope in a tree.

'That must be my lasso. Why didn't you bring it
home, Vic?'

Vic stared at the lasso as if he had never seen it
before. 'I forgot it. Guess I was too excited. The
leopard came down and I was afraid he was going
to come after me.'

'Well, there's no leopard today, so you can rest
easy. Listen. I believe they are coming. They like
this place. Be very quiet so we won't fright-
en them.'

The sambar led the way. The chital came next.
Then Tiny Tim, the little mouse-deer, bunted his
little head against the grasses and pushed his way
in beside his friends.

Vic said, 'Won't they run when they see us?'

'I don't believe so,' said Hal. 'Deer are friends of
man. They are like the dolphin and porpoise that

swim along close to a ship because they like people. Deer don't run from men unless they see guns.'

Hal pulled his lasso down out of the tree. He had a problem. If he snared the sambar, the other two would be alarmed and would run away. He wanted to get all three.

The animals solved the problem. Deer not only like humans, they like each other. The chital, being a little nervous, got as close to the sambar as possible and raised its head so that the two were cheek to cheek. Hal's lasso came flying through the air and settled over both heads.

'We should have brought the truck,' Vic said.

Hal replied, 'We don't need it. Keep very quiet. Let them get used to the rope.'

It was very hard for Vic to stand still. He was very nervous. His heart was pounding away like a sledgehammer. He started to speak but Hal put his hand over Vic's mouth. They stood so for fifteen minutes.

But how about the mouse-deer? It was still tangled in the long grass. It struggled on until it came up beside its big friends.

The boys stood as still as the trees around them.

Then Hal began to pull very gently on the rope. At first the two deer resisted. But the pull was so gentle that it could not mean any harm. They took a step forward, then another, and another. Soon they were walking slowly along without any sign of fear.

Roger picked up the mouse-deer and slipped it into a big pocket of his hunting jacket.

'Good,' said Hal. 'That little fellow is first prize.

I'll bet Dad can sell it for five hundred dollars. So far as I know, there isn't a zoo anywhere that owns a mouse-deer. Any zoo that buys this will have crowds coming to see the smallest deer on the face of the earth.'

Five hundred dollars! It rang like a bell in Vic's head. What couldn't he do with five hundred dollars?

A bush ahead of them came alive. Part of the bush walked out. When had anyone ever seen a walking bush? But there it was, a bundle of twigs, ambling across the path.

The strange sight brought a yelp out of Nervous Nellie. That was the name that Hal and Roger had secretly given Vic. The bundle of twigs was about two feet long.

'Keep away from it and it won't hurt you,' Hal said.

'What is it?' Nervous Nellie stammered.

'A porcupine.'

The things that looked like twigs were the animal's quills. They started at the back of the head and extended far back over the tail, ending in points as sharp as needles.

Vic, fearing the teeth of this beast, stepped to one side and came around directly behind the needles.

'Oh no, not there,' Hal cried. 'That's the really dangerous end of him.'

'You're kidding me,' Vic said. 'I'm safe here.'

'You're not safe. Get out of the way before it charges.'

'Who ever heard of an animal charging backwards? He can't charge unless he turns around, head first.'

'You've a lot to learn about porcupines. I'm telling you, get around in front of it.'

'You think you can fool me,' Vic stormed. 'I'm safe here and here I'll stay.'

Suddenly the porcupine rushed back with the speed of lightning and plunged its needles through Vic's trousers and deep into his legs. He let out a yell that could have been heard a mile away.

The porcupine, well satisfied, disappeared into the bushes, leaving half a dozen of its spines in Vic's flesh.

'So,' said Hal, 'now you see I wasn't fooling.'

Vic wailed, 'Get these spikes out of me!'

'Lie down and I'll try,' said Hal. 'But they are going to hurt a lot more coming out than when they went in.'

'Why is that?'

'Because every spine has a little hook at the end — like a fish hook. That will tear your flesh as it comes out. But we can't leave them in. They're not clean and the chances are they would give you gangrene, then a doctor might have to amputate both legs.'

This horrifying prospect did not do much to comfort Nervous Nellie.

'Both legs!' he cried. 'Why did I ever come to this country? There's nothing here but murder and germs.'

'Don't forget,' Hal said, 'you've done a good deal of the murdering. Think of all those animals you've killed just for fun.'

'It's all your fault,' Vic shouted. 'If you hadn't hired me I'd be all right.'

This was a ridiculous thing to say and Vic knew it. Hal did not bother to answer.

'Now.' He took firm hold of a quill and pulled it out. A tiger couldn't have roared louder than Vic did.

Every quill brought another roar. The hook on each quill not only tore Vic's legs but tore his trousers as well. When they were all out, Hal rolled up the trouser-legs, tore his own shirt in two, and bandaged each leg in an effort to stop the bleeding.

'As soon as we get to the cabin I'll dose these wounds with disinfectant and I think they will soon heal. Get up, and let's move along.'

But Vic was not movable. He wouldn't even try. He was in great pain and, of course, he blamed it all on Hal.

'I'll get the truck,' Roger said.

'There's an easier way,' said Hal. 'Put him on the sambar's back.'

The sambar stood patiently while they laid Vic across the animal's back, his head hanging down on one side and his feet on the other. So they completed their trip to the cabin. Vic was carried inside and the little mouse-deer followed. Going out again, Hal put both of the larger deer into the same cage, knowing they would be happier if kept together.

Then Vic's legs were dosed with antiseptic and he was left to rest until he was able to walk to his own cabin. Hal and Roger went out to feed the caged animals.

Vic noticed that Tiny Tim, which Roger had removed from his pocket, was roaming around inside the cabin. A five-hundred dollar animal — and his for the taking. He picked up the little beast and put it in his own pocket. Somehow he felt better right away. With something worth five hundred dollars in his pocket, his legs didn't hurt so badly after all.

He slipped out of the Hunts' cabin and walked through the woods to his own. His friends, Jim and Harry, were both there. He showed them his treasure. They had never seen anything like it in their lives. It didn't look real — it had the perfect graceful shape of a deer and yet it was the size of a kitten.

'That's what makes it special,' Vic said. 'It's worth five hundred dollars. I'll give a hundred to each of you and keep three hundred. We can have a lot of fun on five hundred dollars.'

'Fun in jail,' Harry said. 'That's where we'll all wind up. And it won't be just for a night. It will put us away for months.'

There was a rap on the door and Hal came in. 'Did you see — oh, there it is. How did it ever get here?'

'Well,' began Vic, thinking hard what to say, 'you weren't in your cabin. I was afraid it might slip out and get lost. So I brought it here — just until you were ready to take care of it.'

'Mighty good of you,' said Hal. He guessed the truth but decided not to say anything about it.

Nervous Nellie had suffered enough for one day. 'How are your legs?' he asked.

'They sting as if they were on fire. Must be that antiseptic you put on them.'

Hal thought, 'You can always trust this guy to say something nasty.'

'Well anyhow,' he said aloud, 'thanks for taking care of Tiny Tim.' He took up the little animal and walked off.

5
The Laughing Leopard

The great sambar deer captured by the boys was as good as a horse.

He was half tame, having been used in the Sherpa villages on the mountain slopes much as the reindeer is used in Lapland.

The sambar had not been bothered by Vic's weight on its back. So Hal wondered if he could ride it.

He took the animal out of the cage. He had no saddle. He had no bridle. He climbed up on the broad back very close to the neck. He gave the sambar a little punch with his heels and was pleased when the sambar began to walk.

But how could Hal make it turn right or left? He could just reach the head. He found that by pressing the head to one side or the other, he could make his mount turn right or left. He practised for some days and became an expert sambar rider. A sort of affection grew up between the man and beast.

One day the headman of a large village just outside

the Gir Forest stopped Hal on his way through the woods.

Tears ran down the old man's face.

'My wife and my daughter have just been killed by a leopard. This devil has killed five hundred and twenty-five of our people during the past few years.

'We have been told that you and your friends are good hunters. Would you come and kill this beast?'

'We'll come,' said Hal. 'We want the leopard — alive, not dead.'

'You'll never take it alive.'

'Well,' Hal said, 'we'll see about that. We'll be with you in about an hour.'

In less than an hour Hal and Roger and Vic were on their way to Gir Village.

Hal rode his sambar. He called him Sam for short. He knew that Sam hated the big cats, because the big cats hated Sam and all other sambars. The tiger and the leopard found the meat of the sambar very delicious food.

But sometimes the sambar beat the cat. One kick from his powerful heels could knock out any animal he didn't happen to like.

Hal rode Sam. Roger drove a Land-Rover and took Vic, who had no liking for this adventure. He would rather have stayed home and nursed his punctures.

Arriving at the village, they found it deserted, except for one person — the headman — also a cow and some goats.

'Where are all the people?' Hal asked.

'Inside their houses. They are afraid to come out. Come quickly, we will go to my house.'

In the house they found the headman's son — but it seemed a cold forlorn place with no wife and no daughter. They had already been buried.

There was a strange man with a knife carving a piece of wood to make it look like a leopard.

'He just came,' said the boy. 'Says he can help us.'

The man turned and bowed. 'I am a magician,' he said. 'I can take the evil spirit out of your leopard. When I get the bad out of him, then he will not do you any more harm.'

Hal asked, 'How can you get the bad out of a leopard?'

'It is easy when you know how,' said the stranger. 'I make this piece of wood look like a leopard. Then I will take it to Katmandu and put it into the river that flows into the Ganges. That is holy water and I will make a prayer that the holy water will take all of the sin out of the leopard. The Ganges will carry the evil spirit far out to sea where it can do no more harm to human beings. And it will only cost you one thousand rupees.'

'One thousand rupees!' exclaimed the headman. 'I have no such money.' He turned towards Hal. 'How much do you charge?'

Hal laughed. 'Nothing at all. All I want is your leopard. I want to take it back to my country where I will teach it good manners. There is no evil spirit in your leopard. The beast just wants something to eat. If we feed it well, it won't go chasing after human beings.'

'I don't believe you can do it,' said the headman. 'But since you charge nothing I'll give you the first chance and if you fail I will try to dig up a thousand rupees for this man of magic.'

'Listen!' said the boy. 'He's scratching every door. No wonder everybody is scared. I hope this door is locked.'

'It is locked,' said the headman. 'He's scratching at it now but he can't get in. We are safe.'

The leopard stopped scratching and broke into a series of coughs that sounded like laughter. 'Har-har-har.'

'He's laughing at us,' the boy said. He was badly frightened.

'Never mind,' said his father. 'He can't get in.'

'Har-har-har!' laughed the leopard. He was not scratching the door now. There was a new sound. The leopard was climbing the outside wall of the house, which was made of sticks and mud. He reached the roof. What would he do now? There was no way to lock a roof. There was a sound of scratching right over their heads. The roof was not solid. It was made of thatch — sticks and twigs and brush.

The boy was white with fear. Vic hid in a corner. Even the magician was terrified. He picked up the wood he had been carving and prepared to swat the beast if it fell into the room.

Now they could see daylight through the roof. The hole grew larger. Hal leaped to the door and opened it. Down fell the leopard followed by a shower of sticks and brush from the roof.

The leopard stood in the middle of the room glaring around him and coughing his 'Har-har-har.'

The magician swung the wooden leopard like a rounders bat but instead of striking the leopard he gave Hal a resounding thump on the jaw.

Things were getting too hot for the leopard. He took advantage of the escape that Hal had provided for him. But he wouldn't go without his supper. He seized the boy and leaped out through the door. A hundred feet away he put down the young fellow so he could laugh again — 'Har-har-har.'

But the joke was on the leopard. Hal came running with the magician's dummy and Roger with a big stick that had fallen from the roof. They attacked the leopard who was not laughing now, but roaring so loudly that doors opened all down the street as people craned their necks to see what was happening. The leopard made off into the woods. The boy limped back into the house, hurt, but not too badly.

Vic came out of his hiding-place in the corner. He stuck out his chest.

'Boy, oh boy, did we scare that leopard. We gave him what was coming to him.'

Of course he had done nothing. 'I'll bet he won't come back.' Vic strutted around like a peacock, enjoying the admiring glances he got from people in the doorways. He was the hero of the hour.

'I'm not afraid of anything that breathes.'

'Well, save your own breath,' Hal said. 'Keep your strength for what will happen when he comes back.'

'He'll never come back,' Vic replied.

And at that very moment the leopard was coming back. This time the animal selected the fellow with the stuck-out chest as his supper. He ran straight for Vic, and Vic ran straight for a tree. He clambered up the tree about twelve feet high and stopped. He ought to be safe here. He didn't know that the leopard is one of the finest tree-climbers in the world.

'Har-har-har,' coughed the leopard. He began to climb the tree. Vic went up too — all the way to twenty feet. The leopard almost caught up with him. Higher, higher, Vic clambered. Now he had reached the top of the tree. The leopard stopped just below him. The animal knew a lot about trees. He was in the habit of carrying any animal he decided to eat up to the highest branches of the trees in order to keep it away from any other hungry beasts. He was so powerful that he could drag up anything even if it were twice his own weight.

But he had had plenty of experience with branches that would break if he loaded them down with his two hundred pounds. So he didn't dare go any farther.

But he would just wait where he was. Sooner or later his supper would come down to him. It was a long wait for both leopard and man. Hal and Roger pelted the animal with stones, hoping it would become annoyed and climb down. No luck. The stones bounced off the strong hide of the animal and fell back down. These falling stones bothered Hal and Roger more than they did the leopard. Several times their heads were soundly whacked and the creature high in the tree laughed.

It was beginning to get dark. Vic's chest did not stick out so far now. He was beginning to whine. As usual, he blamed his trouble on the two brothers. Would he have to stay up here all night? The leopard didn't mind — most of his hunting was done at night. Sooner or later this tasty bit was going to fall straight into his mouth.

Roger had a bright idea. 'The net. I'll get the net.' He ran to the Land-Rover and brought back the net.

'Good idea,' Hal said. With the help of the head-man they spread the net some five feet above the ground.

Hal showed it to Vic. 'Jump.'

But Vic would not jump. 'Don't kid me. I'd break my neck.'

'Jump. We'll catch you. Or do you want to stay

there till morning?' It was getting darker. Soon Vic would not be able to see the net. He finally summoned up what little courage he had and jumped. He hit the net, and bounced up so far that he thought he was going back up to the top of the tree. Then he fell again into the net. It was comfortable there — as good as a bed.

But the leopard was coming down the tree.

Hal had disappeared. He came back with Sam just as the leopard touched the ground. Sam at once did what sambars always do when bothered by any member of the cat tribe. He kicked the leopard with one powerful heel and the beast doubled up in pain. Sam delivered his second blow with the other heel and the big cat tumbled over and lay as if dead.

'Quick,' Hal said. 'Wrap him up in the net and we'll stuff him into the back of the Land-Rover.'

'Thanks for killing him,' said the headman.

'He's not dead,' said Hal. 'He'll be as lively as ever after we get him into his cage.'

The news that the leopard had been captured passed rapidly from house to house and people swarmed out to thank the boys for what they had done. Vic especially enjoyed all the congratulations.

'It was nothing,' he said, 'nothing at all. Any time you want us to help you just let us know.'

Hal cut short his speech. 'No more time for talk. We've got to get this cat into a cage before he wakes up.'

The leopard was still asleep when they got home. The net was removed and the big body was pushed into a cage. When the cat woke up it went crazy trying to break the bars of the cage but it was no use.

The cat settled down over the meat that had been thrown to him. Cold meat! He preferred live meat, warm and juicy. His luck had changed. No longer could he kill, and kill, and laugh his sarcastic 'Har-har-har'.

When morning came, Hal and Roger popped out before breakfast to see their new cat.

The leopard and the tiger in the next cage were talking together in low grunts. It was not a love grunt. These two animals do not care for each other.

The tiger had reason to be proud of his fine black stripes on yellow hide. But the leopard was covered with flowers — at least they looked like flowers. Naturalists called them rosettes, meaning that they were as lovely as roses. Behind them was a soft light-brown skin.

'What a beautiful animal,' Roger said.

'And as brave and strong as he is beautiful,' Hal added. 'Hunters say the leopard is the most hand-some cat in all the Indian jungles.'

'But he has a bad temper,' said Roger.

'I think we can take care of that when we get him in pleasant surroundings on Dad's farm. And any zoo will be glad to give him the care such a beauty deserves.'

'Okay,' Roger said, 'if we can just get him on a ship before Vic steals him.'

Hal laughed. 'To make off with a leopard is not so easy as to pick up a mouse-deer.'

42

6
The Playful Panda

It was a great day when they found a panda.

'Look!' said Roger. 'Away up in that tree. What is it?' Hal took out his binoculars and studied the strange ball of fur.

'My boy,' he said, 'Columbus discovered America. And you have just discovered something that any zoo would give its eye-teeth to have. That's a panda. Dad wanted one. But I never expected to be able to give him one.'

'Okay,' said Roger. 'If it's so great why don't you go up and get it?'

'I wouldn't think of such a thing. You discovered it, my dear Columbus. You are entitled to the honour of bringing it down.'

Roger grinned. 'How generous of you! What's the reason you don't want to touch it? Will it bite?'

'You guessed it. The panda's teeth are like razors.' Hal pulled out some twine from his pocket. 'Tie this around his jaws. Then he can't hurt you — except with his claws.' He saw that his brother was worried.

'I was just kidding,' Hal said. 'You stay here safe and sound and I'll go up and get it.'

'Not on your life,' said Roger. 'I saw it. I'll bring it down.'

Hal was pleased. He wanted to train his young brother to face danger. That would not be difficult. Roger had a lot of Hunt courage.

He climbed the tree. The panda was rolled up, sound asleep. Roger tied the mouth shut. He didn't know what to do about those long sharp claws on all four feet. Just have to take a chance.

He started down with the heavy animal in his arm. That left only one arm to clutch the branches. What if the beast woke up? It would struggle and fight and cut with its four sets of razors.

Then he noticed that the creature's eyes were wide open. The panda was already awake. But it was as quiet during this jolting trip as if it were being rocked in a cradle.

Most animals would have screamed and struggled. But this one didn't know anything about men. It didn't know how cruel men could be.

But it put up one foot and pulled the twine from its jaws. Still it did not bite. It was an instant friendship between boy and beast.

Roger and his burden reached the ground safely. Hal was amazed.

'Friendly little fellow,' he said.

'Not so little. He nearly broke my arm.'

'Well, you were lucky that he wasn't full-grown. When he grows up he will weigh more than a hundred pounds. What a beautiful red overcoat he is wearing. He needs that, because his homeland is

about twelve thousand feet up the mountain. He comes down to eat bamboo shoots.'

'Doesn't he eat anything else?'

'Yes. For dessert he fancies insects, wasps, bees, hornets, and he kills them so quickly between those sharp teeth that they don't have a chance to sting him.'

'I'm going to call him Pan,' said Roger.

Hal lifted one of Pan's front feet.

'See. It's almost a hand, not a foot. Hardly any animal except the monkey has a thumb. This panda can pick up anything between his thumb and what serves as fingers. Try picking something up without using your thumb. You do much better with a thumb. Put him down.'

'He'll run away.'

'No, I don't think so. He likes you.'

Placed on the ground, Pan looked about as if deciding what to do, then climbed up Roger's trouser-leg into his arms.

And so he rode home. He was not put in a cage.

He was allowed to run free inside the cabin or out.

His life consisted of eating and playing.

'He's a clown,' Hal said. 'You remember the clowns in the circus? Well, Pan is the clown of the animal world.'

Pan the clown was full of tricks. News of his arrival at the Hunt camp soon got around and people came from near and far to see him perform.

Pan was part bear, part raccoon. Like a raccoon, he was clever. Like a bear, he could do all sorts of stunts. The difference was that a bear has to be trained to do stunts, but the panda could do them naturally without being trained.

Pan's first adventure was to climb on top of the leopard's cage. That annoyed the beautiful cat. When a leopard is angry it raises its tail as straight as a mast.

The tip of the tail stuck out through the wire and Pan gave it a good yank. What a roar he got out of the bad-tempered beauty.

Now Pan jumped over on top of the cage that held the King of Beasts. The tiger was so large that the tip of his tail was within reach. Pan tweaked it. The tiger did not roar. His purr was as loud as the sound a dozen house cats would make all purring together.

Hal took a chance. He opened the door of the cage just wide enough for Pan to squeeze in. What would the tiger do?

Tigers eat living animals of any size, as small as a rat or as big as a sambar. But the tiger had just been fed and he enjoyed the cute antics of his roly-poly visitor. He licked the furry bear-raccoon as if Pan were one of his own cubs.

'Take him out,' someone yelled. 'He'll be killed.'

But the greatest of cats was not in a killing mood. He let Pan climb up on his back. He didn't mind when Pan playfully pulled his ears.

The clown took a walk along the tiger's back from one end to the other. The tiger seemed delighted to have company.

But the clown had other business. He jumped down and went to the door. Hal let him out.

The clown at once introduced himself to an old headman with long whiskers who was wearing a hat. Pan grabbed the hat and put it on his own head.

Then he hopped over on to a woman's head, tore off the wig she was wearing and put it on top of his hat.

It was the raccoon in him that made him do such things. The raccoon is as mischievous as a monkey, and as clever as a fox. And Pan had these same qualities.

He cavorted around much as a clown does in a circus. He was having a remarkably good time.

Hal brought out a bowl of soup and a spoon. He showed Pan how to use the spoon. Then he passed it to the animal. The clown was a little bewildered. Pandas don't take soup and they don't use spoons.

But Pan was not easily defeated. He took the spoon, dipped it into the soup, then took it out upside down and tried to get it into his mouth.

The result was that he did not get much soup but he did get a lot of laughter from the crowd.

'Now I'll give him what he really likes,' Hal said.

He crumbled some bamboo into small bits and offered them to Pan.

The clown showed Hal just how a panda eats bamboo, his favourite food. He lay on his back and scooped the bamboo bits on to this chest. Then he took up each bit in his front paws that looked so much like hands and he began chewing the hard chunks of bamboo. The crowd looked with astonishment at an animal eating wood. But thanks to sharp incisors and powerful molars Pan made short work of chewing and swallowing the bamboo. Then he rolled up and went to sleep.

Hal saw to it that the old headman got his hat and the woman her wig.

'Great show,' they said.

'Don't thank me,' said Hal. 'It's Roger who got the panda.'

So Roger was thanked by everyone and the guests, still laughing at the performance of the raccoon-bear, went home much pleased with themselves, Roger, and the panda.

7
Runaway Elephant

Vic thought he was a fine-looking fellow and wanted Hal to take his picture half a dozen times a day.

'I want a picture of me on an elephant,' he said. The three boys were in a timber-yard of the Abu Singh Teak Company. They had been watching an elephant pick up a log as long as a telegraph pole, rest it on his tusks, hold it in place with his trunk, carry it across the yard and place it carefully on a pile of logs.

There it would stay until some shipbuilder wanted to build a vessel's hull out of wood that would last a lifetime without decay.

Teak was not very well known in Western countries but it grew well in India up to altitudes of three thousand feet. The trunks made logs that were floated several miles downstream to the timber-yard. The wood was regarded by the Indians as the finest in the world, even better than mahogany.

When the elephant had done his job Vic said, 'Make him lie down. Then I can get on his back.'

'But he's not a riding elephant,' the mahout

objected. 'He knows what to do with logs but he's never had a stranger on his back.'

'Okay,' said Vic, 'then this will be the first time. I'll teach him.'

The mahout brought the animal to earth. Vic climbed up on to the broad back.

'Shall I take the picture now?' Hal asked.

'Of course not. I'm not going to have my picture taken on a lying-down elephant. Make him stand up.'

When the elephant stood the picture was taken.

The click of the camera and the strange feeling of something heavy on his back was more than the elephant could stand. He whirled about, shot out of the timber-yard and raced down the street.

An elephant in motion puts down two feet on one side, then the two feet on the other side, and this makes him roll back and forth. When there's no saddle, the rider has a hard time sticking on.

Vic hung on to the rubbery edges of the two ears and wished he had never tried to ride this wobbly beast.

The mahout, yelling at the top of his lungs, came running after them but could not catch up. Vic rolled about like a peanut on the hurricane deck of this ship of the jungle and expected to be shaken loose at any moment.

The elephant was not accustomed to traffic and took the wrong side of the street. Presently a Ford came straight towards him, honking as if the driver really thought that this mountain of flesh would move out of his way. When it did not, he saved himself and his car at the last moment by plunging through a fence, across a garden, and into a bamboo home. The screams of the people in the house followed Vic and his mount.

And now came a rickshaw, fortunately empty. With one touch of his trunk the elephant flicked it into the gutter, the rickshaw man still cooped between the shafts.

The elephant's trunk was making mad circles in the air. Sometimes it was flung back in Vic's direction like the tentacle of an octopus. How far back could an elephant reach with his trunk? Elephants could shower their own backs. Vic wondered if he would suddenly be picked off and flung into someone's second-storey window.

They arrived at a busy cross-street. In the middle of the crossing was a policeman on a traffic platform operating a stop sign.

But the elephant, though very clever with logs, was not clever enough to read. He surged straight on, with cars, rickshaws and gharries scattering out of the way in a panic. The policeman roared and the general public screamed.

Now the wild beast was carrying Vic alongside a river. But this was hot work, and the elephant decided to take a bath.

First it was only five feet deep and Vic did not worry. But it became deeper and deeper and finally the elephant's back disappeared under water and Vic was soaked to the skin.

The elephant had one advantage over Vic. The animal, though under water, could raise the tip of his trunk above water and thus breathe easily. Vic did not have the same equipment. He could keep

51

his head above water only by standing up on the elephant's back.

Hal and Roger came running along the bank.

'Look out!' Hal yelled. 'You'll drown. Swim to the shore.'

'I can't swim,' came from the miserable Vic.

Just in time, the elephant solved that problem. He came up on shore. Both he and his rider were completely covered with a coat of mud which the elephant's feet had churned up from the bottom of the river.

Hal and Roger ran to help Vic down. Before they could do so the elephant decided to clean the mud off his hide. He threw his trunk back and vigorously sprayed water not only over himself but over the three boys. Vic slid down and joined the other two. They were a pretty sad sight as they stood there, dripping muddy water from their hair, faces and clothes.

But the worst was yet to come. Because insects were stinging him, the elephant scooped up sand and covered himself with it as protection against these little pests. Of course the boys got their full share of the sand in their hair, on their faces and all over their clothing. Now they looked worse than ever.

The mahout had arrived. He could hardly recognise these three disgraceful tramps.

The elephant had quietened down now that there was no one on his back and his mahout was there to take care of him. They all returned to the timber-yard.

'That will be a hundred rupees,' said the mahout.

Hal was surprised. 'For what?' he said.

'For the ride.'

'But nobody wanted to ride,' objected Hal.

'But your friend did ride.'

Rather than continue the argument, Hal paid one hundred rupees. Then he said, 'Now, what are you going to pay us for all the trouble your elephant gave us? He could have killed my friend. He went wild and you had no control over him. Our clothes are spoiled, perhaps ruined.'

The mahout laughed. 'That's just your bad luck,' he said.

'Let me see how much you should pay us,' Hal said. 'I think that one hundred rupees would be just about right.'

'You'll never get it out of me,' said the mahout.

'That's all right,' Hal said, looking at the sign 'Abu Singh Teak Company', 'we'll just report all this to your boss, Abu Singh.'

The mahout was no longer laughing. 'Oh don't do that, please. He would fire me. Here's your hundred rupees.'

He passed back the money to Hal and the three boys went home.

'He wasn't such a bad fellow after all,' Roger said. 'And he spoke our language pretty well. I'm surprised that so many people in India speak English.'

'It's not surprising,' Hal said. 'The British ruled India for three hundred years. They started hundreds of schools and taught English and Hindi in every one. Now that the British have left, India still teaches English.'

'Why?'

'Because English is a world language and India wants to keep up with the world.'

8
The Great Round-up

How do the timber-yards get their elephants?

Hal and Roger were going to find out today.

Wild elephants that roamed the Gir Forest and had never seen a timber-yard were going to be caught and sold later to the teak kings such as Abu Singh of the Abu Singh Teak Company.

Hundreds of 'beaters' would scour the Gir Forest in a search for wild elephants. They would then beat pans and scare the elephants through the forest into a great corral which had already been built. There was room in it for a hundred elephants or more. The corral was surrounded by a fence, not an ordinary fence which the elephants could easily break down, but a fence of great logs, every one of them a foot thick.

Tame elephants, each one with a mahout on its back, would help to drive the wild ones into the corral.

Roger and Hal wanted to see the whole show.

Some of the mahouts were not very kind to their animals. Roger saw one goading his elephant with a sharp stick. He kept it up until the beast became angry. Finally the elephant tossed his trunk, wrap-

ped it around the mahout, and flung him down on the ground with great force.

The mahout's head struck a stone, and he lay as if dead. Roger called Hal.

'See what you can do for this brute. He was hurting his elephant — and he got what he deserved. Perhaps he's dead.'

Hal bent over the unconscious mahout. Blood was flowing from the injured scalp. But Hal noticed that the man was still breathing.

'I'll take him to the hospital.'

Both boys lifted the body and put it into the back of their truck. Hal drove off.

The mahout's elephant was very nervous. He knew what he had done and was afraid of being punished. He trumpeted loudly. Roger put his hand on the elephant's neck and patted him gently while speaking comforting words.

'There, there. It's all right. You did just the right thing. Don't worry. He's not going to prod you any more.'

Although the elephant could not understand what Roger was saying, he did understand the petting and the quiet voice. He was a friend. He stopped his trumpeting and stamping about. He looked at Roger from head to foot. Yes, he could trust this human. He wrapped his trunk around the boy and lifted him to his back.

Roger had become a mahout. He didn't quite know what to make of all this, but he had heard that you steer an elephant by pressing your toes against his neck on one side or the other, depending on where you want to go.

So off they went, boy and beast, both quite content. Roger began looking for a wild elephant that he could drive into the corral.

But things were not going to be so easy for the juvenile mahout. Passing by a bank as high as the elephant's back, he was suddenly aware that he had company. A low growl announced that something had stepped from the high bank on to the elephant's back — something that was fond of elephant meat. Roger looked round, but the shade of the trees was so dense that he could hardly decide whether his new companion was a tiger or a leopard. A shaft of sunlight came through the trees and he saw that his guest was a great brown bear.

His father had asked for a Himalayan bear and here it was. But the bear had arrived at a very inconvenient moment. How could Roger get him home and into a cage? And just how patient would the bear be?

'Not very patient,' Roger thought, 'if that growl means anything.' Shivers ran up and down his backbone as he waited for the bear to come forward and attack him.

But the bear had a problem of his own. He was not used to riding an elephant. The rolling motion of the big beast made it difficult for him to hang on. He was too busy keeping his balance to bother about the boy way up forward on the elephant's neck. He dug his claws into the thick hide and his growl became a roar.

Roger turned the elephant towards home. He hadn't the faintest idea what he would do when he got there. Luckily, it was less than a quarter mile and he soon drew up before the cages.

He wished that Hal was there to help get the big brown animal into a cage. Hal was not there, but Vic was. Hal had told him to feed the animals and he was doing that. He saw Roger — then his eyes travelled back to the great brown beast and Vic took to his heels.

'Come back here,' Roger called. 'Come back and open a cage.'

Vic, trembling, crept back with his eyes fixed upon the bear. If the beast roared he would run again and he wouldn't come back.

'Open the cage door,' Roger said. 'That stuff you've been feeding the deer, put a lot of it in the cage.'

Vic did as he was told. The bear stopped roaring. His eyesight was not so good, but his sense of smell was fine. Here was breakfast all set out for him. With a low rumbling sound that meant a good appetite, he jumped down and entered the cage.

'Close the door,' yelled Roger.

With the door closed and locked, Vic sang a different tune.

'I got him. I got him. Your brother will have to pay me fifty dollars. I risked my life to get that beast. Fifty dollars!'

As usual, Vic took all the credit.

Roger did not stop to argue but, touching his toes to the elephant's neck, he returned to the round-up.

'Where have you been?' Hal demanded rather crossly. 'Can't you stick to your job?'

'I just went home for a bit.'

'Why did you go home?'

'You'll find out when you get there.'

The elephant was wise enough to know that his friend Roger was being scolded. With his trunk he picked Hal up as easily as if the boy had been a feather, and planted him in a mud puddle.

Hal returned to his truck thinking that there was nothing in the world so wonderful as an elephant's trunk.

With his trunk an elephant could breathe, could drink, could shower himself with water or sand, could pick up twigs and use them as a fly-swatter to brush the insects from his hide. He could smell with his trunk, he could gather food and carry it to his mouth. He could clear bushes out of his way, he could purr, he could roar, he could frighten other animals by banging his trunk against the ground, he could seize a tiger or any other enemy, he could whack anyone or anything that got in his way. He could show affection by caressing his mahout with his trunk, and he could plant Hal in a mudhole. The trunk was the most dangerous part of an elephant — and the most useful. Hal was surprised that the elephant had become so fond of his kid brother. But Roger had a way with animals — they all liked him.

Now there was a terrific noise as the beaters came, driving the wild elephants into the corral. The elephant may be big, but he scares easily. The beaters were beating gongs, bells, drums, sending up fireworks that exploded in the sky, and every beater was shouting at the top of his lungs.

When all were inside, tame elephants were sent in, each with a mahout on its back. The job of the tame elephants was to quiet the wild ones and give them their first training. Every newcomer was joined by two tame elephants, one on either side of him. They stuck so close to him that he had to stop roistering around wildly and begin to realise that, although he was a captive, life was not going to be so bad after all. A few days in the corral with his tame companions would calm him down. Then he would not be too excited when a mahout got on his back and continued his training. If the mahouts were kind it did not take more than a few days before the strangers would feel less strange and could start work in the many timber-yards.

In the timber-yard they would quickly pick up the twenty-seven words that every logging elephant is supposed to learn. Each word called for a different action. Of course the elephants could not speak the words, but they could hear them, and with a little experience they could do exactly what the mahouts wanted them to do. It must always be the same word for the same action. If a different word were used, the animals would not understand.

Arriving home from the round-up, Hal was astonished to see a big Himalayan bear neatly caged.

'How did you do that?'

Roger began to answer but Vic cut him off. 'It was a good deal of work,' said Vic, 'and pretty dangerous. But I got him at last. That will be fifty dollars.'

Hal looked at Roger. Roger winked, but said

nothing. Hal guessed it was mostly Roger's work rather than Vic's. But since Vic had not caught anything yet and might be getting discouraged, Hal gave him the money.

From that time on Vic took everyone to see the bear and told them how brave he had been to catch and cage such a monster.

Roger had taken the elephant back to the round-up. He noticed a wild elephant that was dancing about and trumpeting furiously. A tame elephant was on one side, but there should have been one on the other side.

The temporary mahout, Roger Hunt, brought his elephant up where it was needed, and two tame animals pressed closely against the trouble-maker to calm him down.

An hour later Hal showed up. 'You and your elephant seem to be very fond of each other,' Hal said.

'We are,' said Roger, 'and I hate to give him up.'

'You don't need to. He's your elephant. At least until we ship him home to Dad.'

'My elephant? But he isn't mine.'

'I've just been to the hospital to see the mahout,' Hal said. 'He gave me the name of the owner. I went to him and bought the elephant. You remember Dad wanted an Indian elephant. We couldn't get a better one than this. So, until we go home, he's yours.'

'But he must have cost you a mint of money.'

'Not so much. And Dad will be able to get a good price for him.'

Roger was choked up. 'Hal,' he managed to say, 'you're a good guy. This critter put you in a mud-hole. That's enough to make a fellow mad. But you don't get mad. Instead, you do this nice thing.'

'Save your breath,' said Hal, embarrassed. He called to a mahout who happened to be free. 'Want to take over? We're going home.'

The exchange was made. Hal climbed the log fence and perched on their elephant behind his brother. Home they went. All three of them, counting the elephant, were very well satisfied. Big Fella, as they called him, was put into a cage.

'You'll have to get busy and find some fodder for him,' Hal said. 'Big Fella will eat six hundred pounds a day!'

9
The Boy and the Beast

The terrible gaur. It rhymes with power and it rhymes with sour.

Both words describe him well. He had more power than any other member of the wild ox family. And he was as sour as vinegar, grumpy, crusty, cranky, cross and savage.

He stood seven feet high, his two upturned horns were each three feet long, his ears were large, his food was grass, bamboo shoots, twigs and leaves of various trees and bushes.

A headman told the boys, 'When the gaur is attacked it will pick up a stone in its nose and blow it out with a force great enough to kill a man.'

The boys took this with a grain of salt, but they were ready to believe that the gaur was a very bad customer.

'If he gets you on his horns,' said the headman, 'he will carry you for miles, no matter how heavy you are — then he will shake you off and may stamp you to death.'

But Dad had ordered a gaur, and a gaur he should have. How could two boys capture such a formidable beast?

'We're apt to find him anywhere between here and six thousand feet up the mountain,' Hal said. 'We'll use the truck. And we'll take along a pole lasso.'

A pole lasso consisted of a long pole with a loop of rope at the end. With luck, they might get this loop over the wide-spreading horns and then drive back to the cages and stow the beast away.

It seemed simple, but it was going to be very difficult.

They drove around most of the day and it was not until late in the afternoon that they came upon a herd of about a dozen gaur. They selected the biggest one and, poking him with the pole, made him run while the truck ran alongside.

Hal was driving, Roger held the pole. He got the lasso over one horn but the animal shook it off.

The gaur stopped, glaring at the truck, bellowed with rage, and charged.

The great strong horns smashed into the truck which immediately rolled upside down with the two boys beneath it. The animal seemed to think that the truck was alive. Again and again he crashed into it, his horns making deep holes in the iron hide of the monster.

Then he remembered his tormentors and went about, snuffling loudly, bellowing, sending shivers of fear down two backbones. Time after time the angry beast hurled his two thousand pounds against the truck.

Finally he turned the car over and there, in plain sight, were the two boys sitting on the ground.

Now it was just ten seconds before they would

both be dead, unless they acted as fast as lightning.

The gaur came for them, his eyes blazing red, his roar sounding like thunder, but when he arrived the boys were in the truck, now upright, and all he could do was to give the truck some more punishment.

Hal started the truck. The gaur followed close behind, determined to kill this big iron brute and the two humans who rode in it.

There is one animal that is not afraid of the gaur. It is the tiger. There was an explosion in the bushes and the big striped lord of the cat world leaped twenty feet to fasten its jaws on the gaur's neck.

The boys might have been thankful but they were

not. They didn't want a dead gaur. 'Use the lasso,' Hal shouted.

Roger did so but the result was not good. The loop at the end of the pole settled over the tiger's neck.

Just at present they didn't want a tiger. They wanted a gaur. At any other time they would have been grateful for the tiger's help, but not now. Roger pulled lustily. The tiger's jaws relaxed and with the claws of his two front feet he jerked off the noose that was choking him. He gave up the idea of having a gaur for dinner and slunk away into the bushes.

Now the gaur had lost not only some of its power but its sour too. It wasn't chasing the truck with the same enthusiasm.

It was easy to see why. The teeth of the tiger had cut deeply into the neck of the gaur and blood was trickling out.

The beast turned its head to look after the tiger, and this was Roger's opportunity. With its head turned, the three-foot horns and the head were all on one line, and with a flip of the noose the animal was captured.

He was suffering from a deep gash in the neck and had no more thought of charging either the truck or the boys.

He came along with his head hanging down and no more fight in him.

A cage that was too small for an elephant but just the right size for the great hump-backed terror of the Gir Forest was waiting for him.

The noose was still round his neck and the pole

was fastened to the noose. 'How can we get him in?' Roger wondered.

'Go into the cage and stick the pole through the back of the cage, take hold of the pole, and pull. I'll be there to help you.'

Roger did as Hal had suggested. Then both boys went round behind the cage, took hold of the end of the pole, and hauled away on it with all their strength.

The animal did not feel well. At first he resisted, then he moved forward an inch at a time and finally found himself in the cage. Roger ran back to close the door.

'How do we get the noose off his neck?' Roger asked.

Hal said, 'Just leave it there. If he starts to rampage around we can pull the noose tight so that he won't succeed in breaking the cage.'

Just for the moment the great wild ox had no idea of breaking anything. The pain in his neck had quietened him down.

'What do we do about that cut in his neck?' said Roger.

'Let it be,' Hal advised. 'The blood has stopped already. I can squirt some antiseptic on the cut without going into the cage. The tiger's teeth may have been a little dirty. He'll be all right in a few days.'

10
The Crazy-Cat Who Eats Himself

A strange animal came prowling around the Hunt camp. It had a tan-coloured skin.

Roger saw it first. He called Hal. 'What do you think of that? It's striped just like a tiger. Do you think it's a young tiger?'

'No, it's a hyena.'

'You're nuts. We saw lots of hyenas in Africa. They didn't have stripes.'

'I know,' replied Hal. 'But the Indian hyena is a little different. It wears stripes. Dad wanted one of these. Let's grab it.'

'It looks like a kind of cat,' Roger said. 'Here pussy, here pussy. No, it looks more like a dog.' And Roger barked.

'It's a little of both,' Hal said. 'You might call it a cat-dog.'

The hyena began to laugh. 'Ha! Ha! Ha! Ha!' Then he sang a very different tune: 'Garrar! Gurr-rr-aa! Guddar! Guddar! Guddar! Goo-doo! Goo-doo!'

Then the beast made a screaming noise, starting

low and running up high, staying high until it almost split the ears of the listeners, then dropping to low.

Roger looked around. He wasn't sure that all these sounds had come from this beast. The animal had a curious ability to throw its voice this way and that so that no other animal could tell where the sound was coming from.

'What a curious beast!' Roger said. 'It's not just a cat-dog. It has a dog's face, a lion's ears, and the body of a bear. It has the teeth of a tiger. Why doesn't it run? Isn't it afraid of us?'

'It may be afraid, but it smells the animals in the cages and would like to get at them.'

'But I thought hyenas didn't attack live animals. Those in Africa just ate dead bodies.'

'These are a little different,' Hal said. 'They are bolder than the others. The headman of that village we visited told me that a hyena sneaked into a house, snatched up a baby, and ran out. The baby was very much alive and yelled to high heaven. The squalling was so loud that it frightened the hyena. It dropped the child and the mother ran out and got her baby.'

Hal went into the cabin and came out with the lasso. He forgot to close the door. Behind his back, the cat-dog-lion-bear-tiger slipped into the cabin. There was a great crackling, grinding sound and the boys looked in to see the hyena eating a clock. That clock would never go again. The hyena is famous for its terrific jaws. After the clock was ground up and swallowed, the tiger-striped beast saw Hal's best hat on a peg. He stood on his hind

70

legs, pulled down the hat, chewed it up and swallowed it.

Roger laughed, but Hal was not so happy. He threw his lasso. Then he dragged the animal out screaming and screeching like a maniac. The monkeys in the trees set up a wild chattering and the birds joined in. Vic came running over to see what it was all about. The hyena pulled off one of his boots and ate it. Hal and Roger together pulled the beast to a cage. After a struggle in which they both got nipped, the crazy cat was in the cage and the door was shut.

'I don't know why Dad wanted that horrible beast,' said Roger.

'He didn't want it, but a zoo ordered it so he told us to get it.'

The boys went into the cabin. Not only the clock and the hat were gone, but three books on wildlife were in the hyena's stomach.

'Well,' Hal said, 'he has very good taste. Those were excellent books, and it's nice that he appreciated them. I hope they give him a stomach-ache.'

Hal told Roger and Vic of the old local saying that hyenas are usually men or women who have come back from the dead in this form. They had been witches in their previous life and were considered very dangerous. 'But it's just one of those superstitions,' he said. 'The fact is, the hyena is not all bad. It can really get quite affectionate.'

Vic thought he would find out just how affectionate this animal was. He put his fingers in through the wires of the cage. The hyena cocked its head to one side and studied those fingers. Then it leaped

71

forward and clutched the fingers between its jaws. Vic let out a shriek that was as loud as any shriek of the hyena.

Clocks, hats and boots. Better than Vic's fingers. It let go, and Vic drew out a very bloody hand.

Roger came out of the house with a piece of meat. He tucked it in between the wires of the cage and the hyena promptly devoured it. Looking at Roger, it made a sound that seemed very much like a purr. That was the cat in it. Roger knew that he would get along very well with this new neighbour.

'It's all right,' he said. 'It's really kind of handsome with those strips and all. And it smells rather sweet — not like the African hyenas. I think it will make a good pet.' Roger found he could go into the cage and never fear those terrible jaws. He tickled the animal in the neck where dogs and cats like to be caressed, and Hi, as he called the hyena, responded with a noise that was halfway between a growl and a purr. If this hyena had once been a human being, he or she was certainly a friendly character.

One morning Roger found the hyena lying on its side, very sick. He called Hal. The animal was acting very strangely. It was biting its own stomach, chewing its legs until the blood came, and nipping its tail. A living animal eating itself as if it were a dead one!

'They do that when they are about to die,' Hal said. 'But we won't let this one die, I think he just has a bad case of stomach-ache.'

He ran to the cabin and came back with some

alkaline tablets. Roger opened the door just wide enough so he could squeeze in and he fed the medicine to his suffering friend. Ten minutes later the hyena stopped eating itself and plainly showed a desire to live. It brushed up against Roger just as a cat or a dog would do, and Roger petted it, keeping away, however, from those powerful jaws that seemed ready to eat anything that came to hand, including clocks, hats, books and fingers.

11
Friends or Enemies?

When Vic turned up one morning at the Hunt camp he was carrying his rifle.

Hal said, 'I see you have your gun. I heard some shooting yesterday. Were you doing it?'

'Oh no, no. I wouldn't do that.'

'Come on now,' Hal said. 'You were doing some killing.'

'No. I was just taking pot shots at some monkeys. I only got a couple of them.'

'What makes you think it's all right to shoot monkeys? You spent a night in jail for shooting. You promised not to shoot any more. If you're caught you won't get off with one night in jail. You'll go to prison for ten years.'

'Ten years! I suppose you will go to the police and tell on me.'

'Not this time. I'm your friend. The next time you shoot I'll give you a little ride. To the police station.'

'Is that all?'

'Not quite,' Hal said. 'How about that two hundred dollars I lent you?'

'You didn't lend it to me. You gave it to me. I don't have to pay it back.'

'Your memory is not too good. I didn't make you a present of two hundred dollars. You were supposed to pay it back when you got a cheque from your father.'

'Well, the cheque hasn't come yet.'

'I think it has come,' Hal said. 'You're wearing a new suit. You can't buy a suit of clothes with no money.'

'Well,' said Vic, 'you can whistle for your two hundred dollars.'

'If that's the way you feel,' said Hal, 'I'll have to write to your father. Not just about the two hundred dollars. The principal thing he should know about is the way you are breaking the law by killing animals in the Gir Forest and risking ten years in prison.'

Vic laughed. 'Fat chance you have of writing to my father. You don't know his address. Cleveland is a big city. If you just put "Mr Stone" on the envelope, the post office is not going to hunt up the address. And I'm not going to give it to you. There's no way in the world that you can write to my dad.'

'I'm not so sure about that,' Hal said.

There was one way he could reach Vic's father. Vic had spent one term at Western Reserve-Case University. Hal wrote to the dean of the university:

Dear Sir – I enclose a letter to Mr Stone, father

of Vic Stone who spent a semester in your college. His address will be in your records. Would you be so kind as to address the letter properly and mail it to Mr Stone?

In his letter to Vic's father, Hal wrote:

Dear Mr Stone – Your son Vic is working for me. I am afraid he will go to prison for a ten-year term if the police learn that he is shooting wild animals without a licence. The police here are very strict. I like Vic and want to save him from a lot of trouble. He is not completely honest. I loaned him two hundred dollars, and now he says it was not a loan but a present. The money doesn't matter so much as the fact that he is breaking the law and may have to suffer for it. We don't want him to have such bad luck.

When the reply came Hal learned that Vic's father's name was Robert Stone and his address was Parkwood Drive, Cleveland, Ohio, U.S.A. Mr Stone wrote as follows:

Dear Mr Hunt – I am sorry to hear that my son, Vic, is giving trouble. At this distance, I can do nothing for him. He is almost twenty and should be able to take care of himself. He ran away from home and made his mother, already a sick woman, so unhappy that her condition deteriorated and a week ago she died. I want nothing more to do with the brat. I sent him a good cheque, but that will be the last. As to the two hundred dollars, I am enclosing a cheque made out to you for that amount. I thank you for your interest in my son but so far as I am concerned he is dead.

Hal showed the letter to Vic. It was a great surprise to the runaway.

'How did you get his address?'

'Don't worry about that. The thing that should really be very heavy on your conscience is that you speeded your mother's death. I think you should go home now and make peace with your father.'

'Not on your life. If he doesn't want me I don't want him. You were a sneak to tell him about me.'

'I thought he might be able to help you. But he has good reason to be sick of you because of the death of your mother. Now you still have a chance to make good. You are still my friend, and I am ready to pay you for every animal you bring in. Let's forget about all this and shake hands.'

Vic put his hands in his pockets. 'No thank you. I wouldn't touch you with a ten-foot pole. I'll get even with you for this.'

'For what? For keeping you out of prison?'

'I'd rather go to prison than work for you.' And with this final taunt, Vic strode off to the cabin where he lived with Jim and Harry.

Vic growled and moped for two days. Then he said to his two companions, 'I've got it. I've got it.'

'Got what?'

'I've got a way to get back at Hal Hunt.'

'Why do you want to get back at him? He just wanted to keep you out of jail.'

'He's a louse. I'll treat him like a louse — step on him and smash him and his business. And I've figured out a way that we can make a lot of money.'

That sounded good to his two companions.

'How would you do that?' Harry asked.

'Simple. Get him in trouble. Fix it so that he has an accident.'

'You mean to kill him?'

'Perhaps. But anyhow get him into the hospital. And his kid brother too. Put them there for a good long stretch.'

'What good would that do?'

'Keep them out of the way so we could sell their animals and put the money in our own pockets. Hunt reckons that on average his animals are worth a thousand dollars apiece, some less, some more. His dad wants sixteen animals. Hunt says he will get about four animals more than that, making twenty animals altogether. What is twenty times a thousand dollars?'

'Well, it's twenty thousand dollars,' said Jim.

'Right. Wouldn't it be nice to have that divided among the three of us? We could sell the animals to zoos and make twenty thousand dollars.'

'But he hasn't got them all yet.'

'No. Give him time to get them and then put him in the hospital. Of course if he dies we can't help that. Nobody can blame us for that.'

Harry said, 'Why don't you go to work and help

him get all his beasts as quickly as possible? After that we can get him and his brother busted up.'

But Vic was too lazy and bitter to go on working for Hal.

'He'd only pay me fifty dollars an animal. What's that compared with twenty thousand? We can start out by making a thousand dollars right now. When they are off doing some hunting we can open the cage where they keep that elephant they call Big Fella and bring him to our place and sell him for a thousand dollars to some zoo. How about that?'

'What zoo?'

'The headman was telling me there are a dozen zoos right here in India. And others next door in Burma and Singapore. Japan is the big money country now. They would probably pay not one thousand but five thousand at the Tokyo Zoo. What do you say? Are you with me?'

His friends were a little uncertain but such money sounded good.

'I'm with you,' Jim said.

'Me too,' said Harry.

12
Another 'King of Beasts'

The tiger is the 'King of Beasts' — bigger, heavier, stronger than any other member of the cat family.

But the lion is also called the 'King of Beasts' and honoured for his enormous power.

The two kings are widely separated. There are lions in Africa but no tigers. There are tigers in India, but no lions.

Except in the Gir Forest. Once upon a time there were three thousand lions in the Gir Forest. Hunters have killed most of them and when the boys came there were only a hundred and seventy left according to the counter of the Forest Patrol.

Dad wanted a Gir lion — not to kill, but to place in a zoo where it would be protected from killers. People would come from near and far to see it.

But Hal and Roger had almost given up their search for a Gir lion. The lions were hiding deep in the forest where there was no road, no path, no trail.

Luckily, the boys discovered them. They peered at them through the bushes. They saw a family or 'pride' of twelve lions, grandpa, grandma, pa and

ma, aunts and uncles, young ones full of mischief, and babies just born.

There was no fighting here. Lions like each other. Grandpa was going about, rubbing up against every member of the pride as if to say, 'Good morning, my dear' — only he said it with a sort of growling purr.

All except the babies had hunted food all night, and now everyone was well fed, happy together, and ready to sleep all day — then up and out at sunset to find more food.

'What a lovely family!' Hal whispered.

'They'll probably all be killed by guns,' Roger whispered.

'At least we can save one of them,' replied Hal.

'Which one?'

'How about the mother and the little one that is snuggling up against her?'

'But there are two babies.'

'Yes, but haven't you ever heard about aunties? It's lion custom for the aunties to take care of the youngster when the mother is away. Don't worry about the little fellow. Auntie Gir will look after him.'

'See — they're all going to sleep.'

'Yes, this is their time for sleep. But that cub is wide awake. Look — he's coming this way. If you can grab him, we'll have his mother.'

'How come?'

'The mother lion will follow her baby. I'll noose the mother with this lasso just to be sure she won't run away. But it's really the cub, not the lasso, that is going to capture our Gir lion.'

The lioness was standing now, looking after her wandering cub. She walked slowly away from the sleeping family. Hal flung the lasso. It noosed the lioness, but she was too much concerned for her young one to notice.

Roger expected her to roar when he picked up the cub. But Gir lions seldom roar. They have learned from sad experience that a roar tells the man with a gun just where he can find the lion. The Gir lion's only safety lies in silence.

'Carry the cub to the truck,' Hal said. 'Go very slowly. If you get the lioness running she may jerk the rope out of my hands.'

He wrapped the end of the rope round a tree to prevent the animal from breaking into a run. Then to the next tree — and the next. So, tree by tree, they approached the truck.

Coming out on the road where the truck stood, Roger put the cub in the cage that had been brought along for the animal they expected to get.

The lioness leaped lightly into the truck and entered the cage. She made a soothing, snuffling sound over her cub, trying to comfort it, and to tell it that no matter what happened, it would not lose its mother.

Roger closed the cage door. 'I have some biscuits in my pocket,' he said. 'Shall I drop some of them into the cage?'

'No. The cub is too young for solid food. Its mother is giving it some milk. A couple of months from now we can start giving it meat.'

Several times before this Hal had used this method of getting a great beast into a cage. It had all been done without worrying either animal in the least. Some 'take-'em-alive' men use more brutal methods. They force the animal along by beating it, prodding it with sharp sticks, shouting at the top of their lungs to terrify it, and shooting into the air to paralyse the animal with fear.

But in Hal's way of doing it, there was no beating, no prodding, nothing whatever to cause fear. There was only love — the mother cat's love had made her follow her young one.

They drove home. On the way, Roger had some questions to ask.

'This lion doesn't look a bit like the ones we saw in Africa. Why is that?'

'Lions differ according to the country they are in. Much of East Africa is six thousand feet above sea level. So it is quite cold all the year round. The Gir Forest is only about a hundred feet above sea level. It is very hot here most of the year. The African lions have heavy coats to keep out the cold. Lions in the hot country wear light coats. Nature is pretty clever. She tries to make animals comfortable no matter where they live.'

'They're different all over,' Roger said. 'These lions are fatter. Their heads are longer. Their legs look different, and their tails.'

'They have an easier life than the African lions.'

'Do the lions and tigers fight each other?'

'No, they get along beautifully together. They seem to regard each other as cousins, not enemies. They really are cousins, you know. Their hides are quite different, but if you undress the tiger and the lion by removing their hides, you find that their bodies are exactly alike — the same organs, exactly the same bone structure. Even an expert can't tell which is the tiger and which is the lion. Only their skins are different — one plain, and the other striped.'

'But in the Bronx Zoo in New York, I saw a lion with stripes.'

Hal laughed. 'Yes, that could happen. If a young animal has a lion for a mother and a tiger for a father, the youngster will be a tiger-lion. Such a crossbreed is called a tigon. "Tig" for tiger and "on" for lion. Or a liger, "li" for lion and "ger" for tiger.'

'That must have been what I saw — a liger.'

Reaching home, they took the lioness and her cub out of the small cage and put them into the great cage already inhabited by the tiger.

'Is it safe?' Roger asked. 'They might kill each other.'

'Look at them,' Hal said. 'Now the two big ones are sniffing each other, nose to nose. They are friends already. I'm sure the tiger is glad to have company.'

Roger brought some meat and put it into the cage. The tiger looked at it and the lion looked at it. Each politely waited for the other to eat. Finally they settled down to dinner, the lion nibbling at one end of the meat, the tiger at the other.

Hal and Roger walked to their cabin. Near the cabin was the cage of Big Fella, the elephant. The cage was empty. The elephant was nowhere to be seen.

'He's walked out on us!' exclaimed Roger. 'He seemed to like me — I never dreamed he'd up and leave me.'

'No,' Hal said, 'he wouldn't do that. Besides, he couldn't open that door even with the thing that looks like a finger at the end of his trunk.'

'So what?' Roger wondered.

'Somebody opened that door. Somebody forced him to come out and took him away. But who?'

For the answer to that, we shall have to look at what happened while the boys were away.

The three crooks lived in a barn that was not a barn. It once was a place for hay and horses, but now it had been converted into a sort of cabin for visitors.

'They've gone,' said Vic. 'Now's our chance to get that thousand-dollar bundle. Perhaps five thousand in the Tokyo Zoo. Come on. Let's get Big Fella.'

They walked to the cage and opened it. The elephant was not as quiet as a lion. He let out a high, shrill scream like the whistle of a fire-engine.

'There now, don't get excited. No use hollering. Your boy friend is too far away to hear you,' Vic said.

He took hold of the end of the elephant's trunk. Big Fella jerked his trunk away. Then he picked up this rascal and threw him into a thorn bush twenty feet off. This bush is famous for its three-inch thorns, each one as sharp as a needle. It is called wait-a-bit because once you get into it you are held by the thorns and must wait quite a long bit before you can get free.

Now Jim took his turn with the elephant. He kept away from the trunk and went around behind the beast. He twisted the tail of the monster. He didn't know an elephant could kick, but he found out when he was plastered against the back wall of the cage.

It was Harry's turn. He gave the screaming beast a resounding whack with a stick he had picked up outside. A huge foot knocked him down and held him down on the floor. If the elephant had rested all the weight of his heavy body upon the foot, Harry would have become a pancake. But, after all, Big Fella was not a killer. He lifted his foot and Harry made for the door holding his stomach.

Now the three took hold of the trunk and pulled. An elephant's trunk is sensitive and the pull hurt.

Big Fella began to move. They walked him out of the cage and down the road to their barn-house.

'What'll we do with him now?' inquired Jim. 'We've got to hide him somewhere. If we tie him to a tree he'll be found. Or else he'll pull the tree down and escape.'

Harry, still nursing his injuries, had no suggestion.

Vic said, 'There's only one thing we can do. Take him into our house.'

'An elephant — in the house? You can't do that,' Jim said.

'We can, and we must.'

'But we couldn't get him through the door.'

'Of course we could. It's a barn door twelve feet high. He's only nine feet.'

So they opened the door and took their guest with them into his new home.

Then they let go of his trunk and he immediately swung it to knock all three of them down on the floor. With a scream of rage he crashed into the wall which, since this was only a barn after all, was made of boards. The boards broke, the splinters flew, the angry beast plunged through, ambled down the road muttering deep in his throat, and Hal and Roger who had just arrived saw him return to his cage. Then he saw Roger and as the boy came to him, Big Fella put his trunk round him and whispered little grunts and wheezes that said he was glad to be home.

'Now I know who,' said Hal. 'Those three crooks. But why in the world did they want that elephant?'

13
Lion Lost

Someone was pounding at the door of the barn-house.

Vic opened the door. He faced a very angry-looking Indian. He owned the place and had rented it to the boys.

'I noticed that you have a great big hole in the wall. How did you manage to make that?'

'We didn't make it,' Vic said. 'The elephant belonging to the Hunts did it.'

'Then the Hunts will have to pay for it.'

'That's right. You go and see the Hunts. They're always causing trouble. You make them come and repair that hole. I hope it costs them a lot.'

'There's just one thing I don't understand,' said the landlord. 'All the broken pieces and chips are on the outside. If the elephant broke in there all that stuff would be inside, not outside.'

'It was inside,' said Vic. 'but we threw it all out-side. We didn't want that mess in our living-room.'

'You did the right thing,' said the landlord. 'How did you get the elephant out?'

'Through the door.'

'I see his muddy footprints on the floor.' The landlord examined the prints carefully. Then he looked suspiciously at the boys. 'You can't fool me. Those prints show that the elephant was not going from the hole to the door. Instead, he was going from the door to the hole. You must have brought that elephant in through the door. Into my house. For some reason you wanted to hide him.' He wagged his head back and forth as he figured out what must have happened. 'You stole him from the Hunts. You brought him in here so no one could see what you had done. The elephant didn't break in, he broke out. So you are responsible. Repairs will cost you one thousand rupees. And since you tried to fool me, I'll just tack another thousand on to that. I'll thank you for two thousand rupees.'

Vic wished he had told the truth. It would have cost less. Lying can be quite expensive.

'Okay,' he said. 'Don't you worry — we'll pay you. You'll have to wait a little while. We have no money, but some will be coming in, if you will just be patient.'

The boys looked so unhappy that the landlord decided to go easy with them.

'I don't think you fellows are very clever. But perhaps you are clever enough to hammer a few boards over that hole. All you have to do is buy the boards — they won't cost much. That would be better than waiting for you to pay me two thousand rupees — I don't believe I'd ever get it. Fix it yourselves. If you don't, perhaps the police can persuade you.'

The boys didn't like that word, 'police'. Besides,

the cold wind blowing in through that elephant-size hole was not too comfortable. So they accepted the landlord's kind suggestion.

'Next week we'll do it,' Vic said. It would never have occurred to Vic to do what needed to be done this week, this day, instead of putting it off until a later time.

He blamed the Hunts. If they hadn't acquired that elephant the three crooks would not have been able to steal it. So the Hunts were to blame for the whole thing.

The three boys drove their Land-Rover down to the Hunt camp. Vic went into the cabin and got one of Hal's lassos. He tied one end to the car. Then they went quietly, very cautiously, to the cage that housed the tiger, the lion and cub.

Luckily, the lion's head was near the door. Opening the door just a little, Vic slipped the noose of the lasso over the lion's head.

Then they leaped into the car and started it. The lion was pulled out of the cage. She might have roared her displeasure, but she had learned not to roar. The little cub did the roaring but it was only a little squeak. The tiger thundered.

The car dragged the lion down the road. But all was not going to be roses for the three thieves. The powerful lion broke the rope and retreated into a cave.

The boys stopped the car and followed. Hanging from the roof of the cave were dozens of beehives. Jim thought they were old hives without any bees. He smashed one with his stick. At once a swarm of bees descended upon the intruders. From all the hives more came and bees covered the heads and faces and arms of the boys and wriggled down into their clothes. Sharp stings plunged into warm flesh.

These were not ordinary bees. They were killer bees like those which, according to the newspapers, had begun to come up into the United States from South America, causing great suffering and death. The stings were very painful. This particular kind of bee loses its sting in the victim and then promptly dies itself. But for every one that died there were hundreds to take its place.

The boys ran on, hoping to leave the bees behind. They came to a small pool of water. The lion was on the other side. They must wade through the pool. It was not deep — just up to their knees. But their legs from the knees down began to give them a great deal of pain. Why should a little water hurt them? When they came out on the other side they saw that their legs were covered with leeches.

There are many leeches in some parts of India. They are worms that vary in length from one inch to half a foot. These were the large variety. Every leech had a big sucker at one end and a small sucker at the other. In the middle was a mouth with sharp teeth. The leech fastens itself to the skin by the two suckers, and then sinks its teeth into the flesh and drinks blood until it becomes twice its ordinary size. It does not need any more food for a month. And it takes about a month for the wounds it makes to heal.

A curious thing about the leech is that it swims backward. It likes to live in water but it is also at home on land. The wound that it makes keeps on bleeding for days.

The boys forgot their lion and made tracks for home. By this time, all those stings from the killer bees had given them a severe attack of ague and fever.

They undressed and began pulling off leeches from all parts of their bodies where the bloodthirsty worms had crawled under their clothes.

Again, of course, the Hunts were to blame.

'Everything is so big here,' moaned Vic. 'Big bees, big leeches, toads a foot long, big lions, big tigers, spiders as big as soup plates on webs that stretch twenty feet, the biggest panda, the biggest gaur bull, the biggest deer, the biggest forest, the world's biggest mountains and the biggest pests — Hal and Roger Hunt.'

At this very moment, Hal and Roger were learning about rhinos. They had met one member of this species and it was giving them much difficulty. It had one horn, instead of two as in Africa, but it made up for this with enormous teeth with which it ate wait-a-bit thorn bushes as if they were lettuce and could chew up a human whenever it got a chance. The boys wished that Dad had not wanted a rhino.

The one that they were trying to catch frightened them with its terrific rushes, but when it came within ten feet of them it would apologise, turn round, go back, and then make another rush.

The boys had made a pit six feet deep and covered it with grass and bushes, hoping that the

rhino would not notice the cover and would fall into the pit. They stood so that the pit was directly between them and the rhino. If the beast came to attack them he would certainly fall into the pit — or would he?

Their rhino was not as intelligent as a lion and constantly made sounds that told everyone exactly where he was. The rhino is said to make no sound, but that was not true of this Indian giant. He grunted, roared, bellowed, snorted and whistled. It is said that both the tiger and the elephant are afraid of the rhino. He had poor eyesight, but this rhino could dimly see the boys and each time he charged they would step out of the way at the last moment and let him run past them.

That was dangerous too, for a rhino, though half blind, can turn on a penny and then you are not

out of his way, but in it. Every time the animal rushed he almost fell into the pit, but not quite.

He lowered his head as if he were going to spear the boys with his horn. But, unlike the African rhino, he did not use his horn which after all is not really horn but a twist of hair hardened to a point. To attack, he depended upon his mighty jaws.

What looked like iron plates covered his sides. In ancient history Indian rhinos had been used as tanks and are now used in warfare. Protected on both sides by armour, it was almost impossible for an arrow to penetrate a rhino's body.

'He's going to go into the pit this time,' Hal said. There was a crashing of branches and bushes and the rhino fell into the pit.

Then the animal went crazy, thrashing about, whistling, tearing at one side of the pit until he pulled down a great deal of dirt and nearly escaped before the boys could get a noose around him. The other end of the rope was attached to the truck.

Then the truck was started, the rhino was drawn up the slanting side of the pit and down the road

94

behind the truck, still grunting and whistling, to his cage.

Once inside it he changed completely. He was quiet and seemed thoughtful. Perhaps things were not going to be so bad after all. He was fed immediately and that made him take a much happier view of life. If a rhino is well treated he becomes tame in a few days.

Turning from the cage, the boys saw their lion coming down the road. She calmly went into her cage and was welcomed with many squeaks by her little cub.

'Those three crooks must have taken her out,' Hal said. 'Then she escaped from them and came back. Let's go right down and have a talk with those fellows.'

Instead of knocking, they opened the barn door and walked in.

They were amazed at what they saw. Three boys lay on their cots, twisting, squirming, whining, bleeding, and every one with high fever.

Hal had intended to scold. But this took all the scold out of him.

'You poor sons o' guns. Whatever happened?'

'Bees,' Vic said. 'Leeches. Oh, mother of Moses. I wish we had kept out of that cave.'

'Bees!' exclaimed Hal. 'You're lucky you're still alive. Roger, sprint down to the cabin and get that bottle of bee-salve.'

Roger was back in a hurry and the two started sealing the wounds of the three culprits.

'When will you boys ever learn?' Hal said. 'It's trouble-makers like you who get into trouble. You'd have a much better life if you didn't try to be so smart.'

'Guess you're right,' admitted Vic. But in his heart he still blamed Hal for everything that had happened. 'We might have died,' he said. 'If you mean to take care of us why don't you stay home instead of gallivanting all over the place while we suffer?'

Hal did not answer this silly argument but continued dressing wounds. He wondered what dirty trick these big hunters would think of tomorrow.

14
Roger's Tiger

'No hunting today,' said Hal.

'Why not?' Roger asked.

'I've got to look after those three sick guys. They've had a terrific dose of bee-poison — not to mention their loss of blood to the leeches. They are covered with bee-bumps. They have a high fever and a bad case of ague.'

'What's ague?'

'It's a kind of malaria. Chills and fever. You saw yesterday what it did to them. With ague, you shiver and shake with the cold no matter how hot the weather is. Then, all of a sudden, you are boiling and sweating and gasping for air. And if the attack is too severe, you die.'

Roger thought for a moment that dying would be just the right thing for these three hoodlums. But he was ashamed of himself for thinking it, and said, 'Can't you get a doctor? Why do you have to bother about it?'

'There's probably no doctor within a hundred miles. No, it's up to me. We've got some things in our medicine chest that may help them.'

'Well, what will I do all day?'

'Feed the animals. Take care of them. You don't need to worry about those crooks taking one of our animals away. They're too sick to try any tricks today.'

Hal picked up his bag of remedies, and left.

Roger fed the animals — but that didn't take long. He was a very active boy and wanted something to do. Why not take a little ride?

He climbed into the truck, and set out. He didn't expect to meet any wild beasts on the road. He enjoyed the fresh air, and the sounds that came from the forest. There was the chattering of a langur monkey. He heard a whistling sound. He guessed that it was the voice of the bird called the Whistling Schoolboy. Morning and evening, this bird pours out its song while in flight, whistling in a soft, sweet minor key a song that has no beginning and no end.

He heard a peacock give its piercing call from the topmost branch of a giant tree. And he heard other birds that he had come to know — the drongos, golden orioles, and rosy pastors which drank the nectar of the samal flowers. Kingfishers went skimming over the river. A horned owl had settled for the day on a branch of the pipal tree overhanging the stream.

The trees swarmed with fly-catchers, woodpeckers, bulbuls with red whiskers, and three kinds of sunbirds — red, purple, and green.

What a paradise the Gir Forest was for all sorts of wildlife.

He was a happy boy — but not so happy when his engine went dead halfway up a gentle slope.

Roger thought he saw something strange out of the corner of his eye. He turned his eyes full upon it. What he saw made him perspire. A magnificent tiger was lying on a rock at the side of the road. Here the boy was sitting in an open truck that wouldn't go. The tiger could reach him in two leaps.

Roger shivered as if he had some of the ague that afflicted the three crooks. There was nothing to prevent the tiger from hopping into the truck and making a breakfast of the driver.

But the tiger looked very sleepy. He gazed at the boy and the truck with half-closed eyes. He was evidently full of food and had no desire to make a meal of this fine boy.

What had he eaten, and where was it? He had killed something, had eaten as much as he could hold, and left the rest for another meal later.

What he had killed and partly eaten could not be far away. Roger quietly slipped out of the truck, walked up the slope, and then into the forest.

He searched for two hours before he found it — the remains of a chital deer.

Roger knew what he must do. He went back to his truck. The tiger had disappeared. This time the engine came to life and Roger turned about and headed for home.

Hal was not there. He must be at the barn-house. Roger drove up there and walked in.

Hal was tending his patients as they squirmed and wriggled, freezing cold one moment and boiling hot the next.

'Come away for a minute,' Roger said. 'I want to tell you something. I'm going to get a tiger.'

Hal laughed. 'A hundred-and-thirty-pound boy is going to get a five- or six-hundred-pound tiger. That's a good joke.'

'No, I'm in earnest. I've seen the tiger and I've seen the "kill" that he has been feeding on. It was a chital and there's a lot of meat there still. Some time between now and morning the tiger will be coming back to eat more. I'm going to be there, and I'll get him.'

'If he doesn't get you,' Hal said.

'He won't get me. I'll be on a machan up in a tree. I may have to stay there all night. I thought you ought to know, so you wouldn't come hunting for me.'

Hal said, 'Listen, kid brother. You're too young to challenge the king of beasts.'

'I'm going to try,' Roger said. 'If you have any advice to give me, spill it now.'

Hal saw that his brother was determined. 'I wish I could go with you,' he said, 'but I've got to stick here with my patients. If you must go, here are a few tips. Build your tree platform, what they call a machan, about twenty feet up in the tree. Just remember that a tiger can make a leap straight up fifteen feet. If you build your platform at less than fifteen feet, he'll get you. There are some boards near the cabin. You're a good carpenter — I know you'll make a good solid machan so if you go to sleep you won't fall off. Take a sleep-gun with you. And be sure to dress warmly. With the wind coming down from the snows on the mountains, you need to have plenty on in order to keep warm. Take a torch so that you can see the animal plainly when you shoot.'

'Is that all?'

'That's all I can tell you. After you put the tiger to sleep, how are you going to hoist him on to the truck? He'll weigh about a quarter of a ton. I don't know how you're going to do it. I don't believe you can, so why not just give up this crazy idea?'

'No thanks,' Roger replied. 'I'll figure out a way to get him up on to the truck.'

'Take care of yourself. Your mother and father would never forgive me if anything happened to you.'

Roger drove back to the cabin to get what he needed — the boards, nails, a hammer, torch and sleep-gun — also a couple of extra sweaters to put on when the night became cold.

Then he drove back to the kill. He climbed a tree not far from the dead chital, and about twenty feet up he found two level branches that would make a good support for his machan. He got to work at once, but it was sunset before he finished his job.

Then he lay down and rested. But it was a restless rest. He was tormented by the problem that his brother had not been able to solve. Suppose the tiger came and ate, and was put to sleep — what then?

Roger wondered how he was going to get a beast four times his own weight up into the truck.

Suddenly it came to him. He climbed down the tree, went to the remains of the chital, picked them up one piece at a time, and put them into the back of the truck. Then he clambered back to his platform.

He was welcomed by a low growl. It was now quite dark but Roger recognised that growl. It was the same as the voice of the leopard who was already in a cage.

A leopard had found his platform and considered it a very convenient place to spend the night. Roger could not see the animal but the leopard had very keen eyes and was a night animal, quite able to see Roger. It slashed out at his head and came away with its claws full of hair. Roger had wanted a haircut but hadn't expected to get it from a leopard.

He turned on his torch and focused the light straight into the leopard's eyes. This form of attack was new to the leopard and it didn't like it. It backed off to the tree trunk, scratched its way down to the ground and Roger could hear it sneaking off through the bushes.

The boy took his place on the platform that had already been warmed up for him. It didn't stay warm, and it was necessary to put on the two sweaters.

Now there was nothing to do but wait, wait, wait.

No matter how hot the day, a night in India can be really cold. Especially with the snow-covered Himalayas acting like a refrigerator.

Hours passed. Still no sign of the tiger. And no sound. Roger shivered and shifted trying to find a position that was comfortable. He strained his eyes

and ears until they felt like tentacles reaching out towards the truck.

Was it all worth while? It was dinner time. He should be in the warm cabin, eating, instead of chattering like a monkey waiting probably for nothing to happen. Hunting was not all it was cracked up to be.

At midnight a tired old moon rose to look in on his foolishness. Its weak light revealed a clearing as quiet as a morgue.

Roger dozed — then was wakened by the excitement of birds. Looking into the clearing he saw a massive shadow approaching the truck.

Swiftly and painfully he got his gun into position. Thanks to moonlight he could dimly see the tiger leap into the truck and begin to eat. Roger turned on his torch and fired the sleep-gun. His aim was good. It was not a difficult shot because the animal was so large that you could hardly fail to hit it.

The tiger roared. All the creatures in the forest screamed. The great beast stood for a moment, then his legs gave way under him and he slumped to the floor of the truck.

He struggled again to a standing position and looked about to find his enemy. Suppose the medicine in the dart had just numbed him and he would not fall asleep? The tiger was no longer interested in the kill. Roger was the kill now. He had been the hunter, now he was the hunted. That was not Roger's idea of adventure at all. A hunter should make things happen, not sit dumbly in a tree and wait for something to happen to him.

It was terrible — that waiting. The pipal tree where Roger had built his machan seemed to tremble although there was no breeze. The local people used to say that this constant movement of pipal leaves was due to evil spirits that inhabit the tree. A more scientific explanation is that the pipal leaf has a long twisted stem like that of the aspen, and quivers in the slightest breath. But Roger thought that the tree was shaking because he was.

Roger used his torch again. Now the tiger was lying down and there was no doubt about it, the gun had put him to sleep.

Roger had found a way to get the big heavy beast into the truck and he had done it without raising a finger. In fact, the dead chital had done it for him. Because the remains of the chital had been put into the truck the tiger had leaped in of his own accord and was now sound asleep and ready to take a ride to the camp.

Roger came down, leaving the platform for the

leopard. Dawn was breaking as he drove home with his valuable cargo.

Hal had just returned to the cabin after his long night vigil. Roger backed up the truck to the open door of a cage. It was just in time. The tiger was waking up. He stood, still very sleepy and unsteady, but when the two boys got behind him and pushed, he did manage to move. He wobbled off the truck and into the cage. The cage door was closed.

'Wonderful!' Hal said. 'How in the world did you get him up off the ground into the truck? You're a strong boy, but not that strong. How did you do it?'

Roger smiled. 'It's a secret. But I'll tell you since you're my brother. You just use a little magic. You say, "Abracadabra, abracadabra," and the tiger is on the truck.'

15
Roger Goes to Jail

'Dad wanted a tiger,' said Roger. 'We got two for him. So we don't need any more tigers.'

Hal did not agree. He said, 'Every zoo that amounts to anything wants a tiger. And they will pay a lot to get the world's greatest cat. Dad can sell all the tigers we can find. But we want other things too. How about just riding out to see what can be found?'

'Will you go with me?'

'Afraid not. Vic almost died last night. The others aren't much better. I'll have to stick around.'

Roger said bitterly, 'Too bad you have to waste time on them. They're not worth it.'

'You don't mean that,' Hal said. 'Even if they were dogs you wouldn't want them to die.'

'But they aren't dogs,' Roger protested. 'They aren't as good as dogs.'

Hal knew how Roger felt. The boy had been up all night. No wonder he was a bit cross.

Big brother went to take care of his patients — who would never thank him for his trouble. Roger got into the truck and drove off, looking for — what?

After more than an hour of driving, the 'what' that appeared was a golden cat.

Roger had been reading about the golden cat in his brother's *Dictionary of Wildlife*. It was a very rare and extremely handsome animal. Hunters who had come before him had spent months looking for one without success.

According to the book, the golden cat would become very affectionate with its owner, but was always savage in the forest and the villages. It was very powerful, with sharp claws and teeth. It preyed upon sheep, goats and even buffalo calves and birds.

The one he saw before him looked like a solid chunk of gold. Its golden coat glowed in the sunlight. It had no stripes, no rosettes, it was just pure gold. And it was worth pure gold. There was one in London Zoo that had been shown on a television programme, a beautiful and magnificent cat. Most zoos were not rich enough to buy one. And usually there was none for sale.

Dad had not asked the boys to get a golden cat, because he knew it was almost impossible. And yet, here was one gazing curiously at the truck and Roger as if he were only waiting to be taken.

Here was a job for the sleep-gun. Roger aimed very carefully and fired. The little dart pierced the skin so lightly that it was not even noticed. The sleep-gun makes no noise, and does no damage. It just makes the animal curl up and forget the world. The sleep lasts about half an hour.

The fine four-foot-long bar of gold stood for a

moment still gazing, then sank down and snoozed.

Roger went to see whether the animal was sound asleep. He touched the cat with the toe of his shoe and there was no movement. He took out the dart and threw it away.

How could he get this beauty into the truck? He would have to carry it, but it probably weighed more than he did. However his weight didn't matter so much as his muscles, and they were strong. He was a little nervous as he looked at those sharp teeth and long claws.

He was about to reach for the cat when a snarl came from the bushes and another golden cat rushed out and stood over the sleeping one. This must be the mate. He need not have had any fear that the second cat would charge him, since the cat was only interested in protecting the one asleep.

Roger sent a dart into the cat's flank. For a

moment nothing changed. Then the second cat settled down over the first, both asleep.

What good luck! Two goldens instead of one! Roger very carefully put his arms around the top cat, carried it to the truck, and put it in the cage. Then he did exactly the same with the other.

We was ready to go home with his booty when a police car drove up and stopped beside the truck. A gruff voice demanded, 'What's going on here?'

The policeman got out of his car and looked at the two animals in the cage. He saw the gun in Roger's hand.

'So, you've killed two golden cats.'

'I didn't kill them. I just put them to sleep.'

'You've killed two of the finest cats in the world. Don't you know that the Gir Forest is a sanctuary for wildlife? Anybody who shoots game here will go to prison.'

'This is not a gun for bullets,' Roger said. 'It just uses a little dart to put an animal to sleep.'

'A likely story!' He peered into the cage. 'Where are the bullet holes?'

'You won't find any bullet holes. These cats will wake up before we get to the police station. I know that's where you want to take me.'

'You are making things worse by lying to me,' said the angry officer.

'Let me explain,' Roger said. 'My father is a collector of wild animals for zoos. He sends me and my brother out to get the animals. We have special permission to hunt in the Gir Forest.'

'Do you have a hunting licence?'

'Yes.'

'Let me see it.'

'My brother has it.'

'Then it's his licence, not yours. I've had enough of your lies. Come along to the station.'

As they went into the station Roger said, 'Your sergeant knows us. He will explain everything to you.'

The policeman snorted. 'He's gone. I'm the new sergeant. And believe me, you're going to get the limit for what you are doing — hunting without a licence.'

'The licence was made out by the Chief of Police in New Delhi. It gives my father, John Hunt, and his sons, the right to take animals from the Gir Forest for zoos where they will be protected and aren't likely to be shot by hippies roaming around in the forest with real guns. My brother is taking care of three fellows who are very sick because they were stung by bees.'

'Stung by bees!' scoffed the sergeant. 'Bee-stings don't make you sick.'

'These were killer bees. They not only make you sick, they may kill you.'

'Another tall story! I've been stung by bees and you can see that I am very much alive.'

'These were bees of another kind. One of the fellows who were stung nearly died last night.'

'Do all the people in your country lie the way you do? It's been nothing but lies since I saw your two dead cats.'

A snarl was his answer, and it didn't come from

Roger. 'You think the cats are dead, take a look at them now.'

The sergeant went to the door and looked. The two cats were awake and active, rubbing up against each other affectionately.

'Those are very valuable cats,' the sergeant said. 'Did you think you could steal them and get away with it?'

'I tell you I had a permit, or, rather, we did — the whole family. Will you let me use the phone?'

He telephoned Hal who was taking care of his three patients.

'Hal, I'm in the police station. They won't believe that we have a permit. Can you bring it up here right away?'

'But I'm busy.'

'If you don't bring that permit up here I'll end up in prison. They accused me of stealing — well, I won't tell you just what. I want you to see for yourself when you get here. It's something wonderful. Be sure to bring the permit.'

Hal grumbled, 'What stupid thing have you done to get yourself in jail?'

'I've picked up two — you'll see when you get here.'

'All right. I have some things to do first. Then I'll borrow the Land-Rover that belongs to these three fellows and I'll come up. It may take a couple of hours.'

Roger spoke to the sergeant. 'My brother will be here in two hours — with the permit. May I sit here in the lobby until he comes?'

'You may not. It's for guests, not for crooks. You'll

111

step into that cell. It may be a bit buggy, and I hope it is. You're probably going to get something a lot worse than that later on.'

The cell was more than 'a bit buggy'. Rats, cockroaches, bedbugs and fleas were Roger's companions. The two hours seemed more like six.

Finally Hal arrived.

'I'm Hal Hunt,' he said to the sergeant. 'Can you let my brother out now?'

'Not until I see the permit.'

Hal stared. 'The permit! Oh, I forgot to bring the permit.'

Roger called from the cell, 'Who's stupid now?'

'Never mind,' Hal said. 'I'll go right back and get it. I'll see you again in two hours.'

The indignant sergeant said, 'I don't believe you have any permit. And I'm not going to wait for you to come back. It's time for me to go home. Bring the permit tomorrow morning.'

'But you're not going to make my brother stay in that lousy cell all night?'

'Yes, and I hope he enjoys it. He likes wildlife. He'll find plenty of it in that cell. And in the meantime I'm going to let those two cats loose.'

Hal had already seen the cats. 'If you do that I'll sue you for a million rupees. Those are two of the most wonderful cats in the Gir Forest. We have a permit and I'll bring it tomorrow morning.'

'Not tomorrow. I forgot, I'm going to be off for three days.'

'That's hardly fair, is it? To keep him in jail for three days when he hasn't done anything wrong?'

'Anything wrong! He's lied and lied ever since I

caught him. He'll stay right where he is for three days. And if there is a permit, and I doubt it, bring it round.'

Hal saw that there was no use in arguing further with this stiff-neck. He knew that he must get those two wonderful animals home or they would be lost.

He drove the truck to the camp and put the golden beauties into a larger and more comfortable cage than the one on the truck.

Three days later Vic was well enough to go with him to the police station and show the permit to the sergeant.

Roger's cell was opened and the boy walked out. His face was covered with the bites of ticks, bedbugs, fleas and mosquitoes, so that he was as sorry a sight as the three hippies had been after their bout with the bees. Hal drove him home in the truck and Vic drove the Land-Rover.

But what a happy homecoming for the three-day prisoner. He was glad to see his cats and they seemed glad to see him.

'Won't Dad be surprised,' Roger said. 'Two golden cats worth their weight in gold.'

16
A Camel Named Jeremiah

'There are no camels in the Gir Forest,' Hal was told by his friend, the headman of the Gir Village.

'But I saw one yesterday,' said Hal, 'and I'm going to get him today.'

'Are you sure it wasn't a sambar?'

'No,' Hal said. 'We have a sambar here. It doesn't look a bit like a camel. The animal I saw was exactly like the ones we have seen in Africa, except that in Africa the camel has one hump and here it has two. I have seen plenty of the one-humped camels and that is the kind they have in most zoos. But a zoo would be lucky if it could get this Bactrian camel that is found only in Western Asia.'

'But we don't have camels in the Gir Forest.'

'You have this one. I think he's a stranger. Probably he came over from Tibet by a pass through the mountains. But he seems to be very much at home here, eating the sort of food that camels like — twigs, thistles and thorns.'

'No animal eats that kind of stuff.'

114

'I'll bring him in and you will see. They will eat cloth, old mats, baskets, newspapers, umbrellas, anything that can get down their throats.'

'Are you just joking, or is this all true?'

'You will see for yourself if I can bring him in. Of course I am speaking of the ones I know — those in Africa. But I have read that these two-humped beasts are the same so far as their food is concerned. I'll try to bring him in. Wish me luck.'

The headman smiled. 'My dear friend, I do wish you luck. You have brought luck to my village by taking away the leopard that was killing so many of my people. I think you are mistaken about the camel. Perhaps it was a yak that you saw. But, anyhow, I wish you all the best.'

Hal set out in search of his camel. He took along some old magazines. They ought to make a pleasant breakfast for a hungry camel. He put a lasso over his shoulder. It would serve as a bridle to lead the camel to the camp where it could feast on more magazines.

He found the camel very close to where it had been the day before. He approached it quietly. The camel saw him but did not stir. This was no wild beast. If it had come from Tibet it would be used to people and as tame as a horse or a dog.

Hal offered it a copy of the *National Geographic Magazine*. The camel at once became a subscriber. It chewed the magazine to a pulp and swallowed it.

Just where it went is a mystery. The camel has

several stomachs and how it chooses one or another is not known.

All the magazines Hal had brought were eagerly accepted and the big brown eyes told Hal that he was a good guy and the camel would love him so long as the supply of such dainties lasted.

Hal slipped the noose over the camel's neck and led it back to camp. Vic was there, probably planning to steal something more from the Hunt menagerie.

He laughed when he saw Hal walking, leading the animal.

'Why don't you ride it?' he asked. 'I'll bet you don't know how to ride a camel. You do it just the way you ride a horse. I've had a lot of experience riding horseback.'

'Fine,' said Hal. 'Then perhaps you'd like to take a ride on this camel.'

'Sure. Why not? I'll show you how it's done. You sit up there on one of those humps.'

He came close to the animal and looked up at the front hump. It was six feet above his own head.

Hal kindly suggested, 'Perhaps you meant between the humps.'

'Yes, yes. That's what I meant. Between the humps.'

But the dip between the humps was still five feet above Vic's head.

Hal encouraged him: 'Jump up and take a ride.'

Vic jumped. He was not much of a jumper. He went up only a couple of feet and came down hard.

'You've got to have stirrups,' he said. 'Every saddle horse has stirrups.'

'Well, this one doesn't have stirrups.'

'Then what can I do?'

'I'll try to get him down for you,' said Hal. He put his hand on top of the camel's nose and pushed down. He said, 'Down. Down.' He had no idea of the Tibetan word for 'down'. The camel, of course, did not understand him. But it did understand that pressure on its nose. It came down to earth.

'There,' said Hal. 'All you have to do is to hop on.'

Vic tried hopping but it was no use. The lowest place in the camel's back between the humps was about level with his head. Vic tried and sweated, and sweated and tried. His face was getting purple with the effort.

Hal picked up a pole and put it in Vic's hand.

'What's that for?' Vic demanded sourly. 'Do you think I'm going to climb up that pole?'

'Not exactly. But you were in college for one semester. In the gym you had to do the pole vault.'

Vic didn't want to confess that he had never been in the gym. He didn't know what to do with the pole.

'If you think it's so easy, do it yourself,' he said.

Carrying the pole, Hal backed off a hundred feet, then came running. He used the pole to hoist himself into the air and sat down between the two humps. Then he slid to the ground.

Vic laughed scornfully. 'That's nothing. Anybody can do it with a pole.'

117

'Then you do it,' said Hal.

Vic took the pole, retreated a hundred feet, and then came on the run. The lower end of the pole was supposed to go into the ground. Instead, it went into the camel. Vic followed, hurtling into the camel's flank. The camel, groaning, swung its head around and gave Vic a good bite on his shoulder.

Vic looked utterly defeated. Hal was sorry for him. He said, 'I'll give you a hand up.' He linked his hands together, making a cup into which, with some difficulty, Vic placed one of his feet. Then

Hal lifted him so that he could get to his place between the two humps.

'See?' said Vic. 'It's easy when you know how.'

The next thing was to get the animal up on its feet. The camel has a very weird way of getting up. It rises first on its hind legs. This would be quite all right except that the beast is still down on its front knees. Vic was thrown violently forward. He threw his arms around the front hump and hung on for dear life. But dear life wasn't good enough. Now the animal came up on its front feet with such force that Vic was tossed in a back-somersault that landed him on the ground behind the camel. The annoyed camel added insult to injury by kicking him in the midriff.

So Hal brought the camel to earth again and hoisted Vic to its back. The camel was peeved by all this folderol and gave him a nip on the other shoulder with his great yellow fangs. Such a nip can be fatal, thanks to blood poisoning from those dirty teeth.

Hal removed the lasso and replaced it with a cord that would serve as a halter. Vic gave the beast a kick with his heels and his mount repeated the terrific toss backward and forward as it rose, then started to walk.

Past experience on horseback did Vic no good. The motion of the camel was a complete surprise. It was a violent catapult forward, then backward. The wave passed up the spine like the crack of a whip. His neck became tired from the effort of his head to stick to his body.

Hal heard the camel gargling as he went along.

The gargling sounded as if the beast were trying to say 'Jeremiah'. So Hal promptly named the animal Jeremiah.

Jeremiah had no bridle. When Vic wanted the animal to go to the right he laid hold of the cord and pulled the beast's head to the right. Then the camel went where he pleased, anywhere except to the right. When Vic wished him to go to the left he pulled Jeremiah's head in that direction and nine times out of ten the camel went to the right.

The camel did not need to see where he was going. He would plod calmly along while turning his head completely round to look at Vic with his great sorrowful eyes, or putting his head upside down beneath his body to bite at a fly.

Finding the cord unsatisfactory, Vic began to use his toes. To do this best, Vic took off his shoes. He wriggled his toes against the left side of the camel's neck for a right turn, and on the right side for a left.

It didn't work. Nothing worked. The animal went where he could get the best thistles and thorns.

Evidently Jeremiah did not need water. Vic could hear a great sloshing of bilge water below decks. Jeremiah's water reserve pitched back and forth in his stomachs and occasionally some of it came bubbling up in his throat. He did not seem to worry about this in the least. No doubt he was proud of what he could do with water. He could store enough of it to last him for a week or ten days. He could store food as well, packing it in his humps in the form of fat. If the humps were high and hard, as Jeremiah's were, it meant that the animal was well fed. At the end of a long journey of a month or so, with little food, a camel's humps drooped like empty bags.

Finally Jeremiah remembered those delicious magazines. He turned about and went back to camp. Hal had the latest editions ready for him. This was a sort of dessert after the twigs, thorns and cactus. He gargled his thanks.

Vic slid down from his mount. Hal had some antiseptic ready for the bites on Vic's shoulders. Vic complained, 'That dope hurts worse than the bites did.'

He went home to tell Jim and Harry how he had conquered the wild beast. They complimented him on his courage and skill.

Harry said, 'I predict that the names Jeremiah and Vic Stone will go down in history. They will be remembered for all time.'

Vic said, 'That sounds good. Would you write it down.'

Harry wrote it and gave it to Vic.

Vic said, 'I'll frame it.'

17
Troubles of a Wild Boar

'We were told to get a wild boar. Let's hunt for one today.'

'What are wild boars like?' Roger asked.

'They are very dangerous animals. A wild boar is a huge pig weighing six times as much as you. It has a very bad temper. You can't depend upon it to be nice and polite. It hides in the bushes and when any other animal or man comes along it rushes out and kills.'

'That doesn't sound good. Can't we just cross that off the list?'

'Hardly. We were told to get it and we'll get it.'

Hal was not aware that just outside the door Vic was listening.

'How will we get him if he's so savage?' Roger asked.

'I don't know. Perhaps he'll get us. We'll take along the sleep-gun and a lasso and hope for the best.'

Vic went back to the barn-house and got his rifle.

'Why the rifle?' asked Jim. 'You know shooting is forbidden.'

Vic laughed. 'Nobody can tell me what to do or

what not to do. The Hunts are going after a wild boar. If they find one they're not going to get it, because I'll shoot it first — just so they won't succeed. They're not going to get a wild boar today.'

'Why don't you let up on the Hunts? You'll only get yourself in trouble.'

'Me? I know what I'm doing. I'm good with a rifle.'

'Are you? That's news to me,' said Jim. 'I'll get your bed ready.'

'What's this about a bed?' Vic demanded.

'I've a notion that you will need it before the day is over.'

Hal drove the truck to a place in the forest that he thought was just the sort a wild boar would love. There were many trees, but also much undergrowth — hundreds of bushes where wild boar would like to hide until the moment came to charge upon any intruder.

Very carefully watching both right and left, the boys crept through the woods. Their nerves were taut. The great tusks of a boar might at any moment sink into the flesh of one of them. And when the beast had finished one boy, he would probably turn on the other.

The boys were not far from their cabin, but it seemed a million miles away. Would they ever get back to it?

Then they saw it — a huge beast with a long nose and savage teeth, two of which were too large to be contained in its mouth. They were the murdering tusks. The animal was turning up the ground hunting for juicy roots. Hal prepared to use his sleep-gun.

Before he could do so there was the crack of a rifle. Whoever had fired was not a very good shot. The bullet passed over the animal's back, only scratching his skin.

Immediately the boar charged — not towards the Hunts, but towards Vic Stone who had dared to fire at the lord of the pig world. Vic yelled to high heaven as the long sharp tusks dug into his side. Then the boar, quite satisfied that he had killed his enemy, started to amble away.

Hal fired his sleep-gun. His aim was correct but the boar did not fall at once. Instead, he glared about, trying to see where that tickle in his flank had come from.

He saw nothing but a viper. The boar is not an animal of great intelligence. Perhaps this snake was the cause of his trouble.

He seized the snake in the middle and started to eat it. The viper turned its head and stung him on the lips. Again and again it attacked him. The terribly poisonous snake was conquering the great beast. The wild boar sank down and died. His death had not been caused by the sleep-gun, nor even by the rifle.

But Vic, suffering from his wounds, took the credit. He and his trusty rifle had killed that monster — so he thought.

He staggered to his feet. He had to get home quickly and lie down. He could hardly walk.

'Take him home on the truck,' Hal said to Roger. Roger did so.

Jim was not surprised to see the great gunman limp in and fall on his bed. He stripped off the fool's clothes and did what he could to stop the bleeding from two holes in Vic's side.

'I was waiting for you,' Jim said, 'but I didn't expect you back so soon.'

'It was all Hunt's fault,' Vic mumbled. 'If he hadn't gone after a wild boar I wouldn't have been hurt.'

Roger drove back to find his brother in a new fight. Another boar, perhaps of the same family, had come running, only to be stopped by another snake. Hal was learning that this particular woodland was the home of many serpents. This one was not a viper. It was a twelve-foot-long boa constrictor. It resented being stepped upon by the big brute. It flung up its head over the neck of the boar and proceeded to coil itself all round the big body. But, unlike the viper, it did not sting.

'What is it trying to do?' Roger asked.

'Well, it's a constrictor. That means it's a squeezer, not a poisoner. It will try to squeeze the boar so tightly that it can't breathe. If we want that boar we have to move fast or he'll die before we can get him home.'

Several men had now appeared from the nearest village. They had seen many strange things in their lives, but this was the first time they had seen a snake hugging a boar.

Hal said, 'Help us carry this animal out and put him on the truck.'

'But how are you going to get the snake off him?'

'We'll just leave it on until we get him in the cage — if he doesn't die first because he can't breathe.'

The men helped carry the beast and its wraparound snake and put it in the truck. Then they all hopped aboard because they wanted to see what would happen next.

Reaching home, they helped unload boar and boa and put them in a cage. Hal said, 'We've got to get that snake off before it kills the boar.'

The men pulled lustily but they could not budge the snake. Something must be done at once. The boar was dying.

Roger had an idea. He backed the truck up to the cage door. He tied one end of Hal's lasso to the truck and put the noose at the other end over the snake's head and drew it fast. Then he got into the truck and started the engine.

What men could not do, the engine did. Inch by

inch, it pulled the snake free and the beast could breathe again.

'Do we keep the boa or let it go?' Roger called.

'Let it go,' Hal said. 'We don't need a boa.'

Roger removed the noose from the boa's neck and let the snake wind away through the forest.

Hal went to the barn-house to see whether Vic was alive or dead.

Vic was sufficiently alive to wail loudly about the trick that fate had played upon him. When he saw Hal he said, 'I'll get you for this. It's the last trick you'll ever play on me.'

'Just what trick did I play on you?'

Vic mumbled and wept and went to sleep, probably dreaming about the terrible vengeance he was going to inflict on Hal Hunt.

18
Midnight Monster

The headman of the village of Bahru dropped by to see the take-'em-alive men, Hal and Roger.

'A rogue elephant is giving us a lot of trouble. It has trampled down our sweet potato crop, smashed some of our houses, and killed several of our people. Can you help us?'

'What does he mean? What's a rogue elephant?' Roger asked his brother.

'Once every year a bull elephant is likely to go "musth".'

'What is musth?'

'It means wild, crazy. The elephant becomes savage. He tramples down the fields, kills the farmers' pigs, kills any people he can reach, and makes himself a deadly nuisance. It lasts for a week or so. Usually he is all right after that, but you just can't be sure.'

The headman said, 'In a week or two we may all be dead. If anything is done it must be done right away.'

'What time of day does he bother you?'

'At night.'

'All right. We'll be on the job tonight.'

'A thousand thanks. I know what you did for Gir Village. That is why I came to you.' And the headman went home with the hope that the killing and destruction in his village would be stopped.

'I don't see how we can do anything with a crazy elephant,' Roger said.

'Let's go and pick a good spot near the village. We'll gather sticks and logs and pile them up so we can set them on fire about nine o'clock this evening. We'll also build a boma — you know, a wall made of thorn bushes that we can hide behind and watch the animals that come out to see the fire. Just like humans, they are curious to see what is going on. Perhaps the rogue elephant will be curious too.'

'But how are you going to tackle him if he comes?'

'I don't know. Perhaps he will tackle us. It's a pretty dangerous business, and I'd like it better if you would stay home.'

'Stay home, nothing! If you can stand it, I can,' said Roger.

'We'll take along a chain and perhaps we can chain one of his feet to a tree.'

'But he could pull down a tree.'

'Not if it's a big tree, and the chain is tied round the very bottom of the trunk.'

'But we have an elephant — we don't want another,' objected Roger.

'No, we don't. Any ship's captain would object to two six-ton monsters. One is all we can ask him to take.'

'Well then,' Roger said, 'if we don't get anything out of this, why do it?'

'Just for the people in that village. But I think a lot of animals will show themselves. We might get one of them. Anyhow we'll take a cage along. We seem to do pretty well with cats — so perhaps we can snare another cat. But whether we do or not, I'll be satisfied if we can save that village.'

Just outside Bahru Village they built their boma. It was made of wait-a-bit thorn bushes. It was about six feet high and a foot thick. Behind this they could hide and watch. Any animal coming up against those thorns would think twice about coming farther. Beside the boma was a tree to which they hoped to chain the elephant — if he appeared. In front of the boma, fifty feet away from it, they piled brush, sticks and logs that would make a good bonfire after they set a match to it at nine o'clock.

They came home for dinner — 'Perhaps the last we'll ever have,' said Roger.

'Oh, don't be so gloomy,' Hal said.

'I was just kidding,' said Roger. He was much excited about this adventure.

'Put on warm clothes,' said Hal. 'It will get pretty chilly during the night.'

'But we'll have a fire.'

'Yes, but it will just warm our animal guests — not us. We'll shiver behind our boma. I'll carry the chain. Do you think you can carry a cat-size cage?'

'Sure. But I think we'd better take the truck. If we do get anything in the cage it might be pretty heavy to carry home.'

130

At nine they drove to the boma. They started the fire. Roger made two holes through the thorn bushes so they could see if anything came prowling round the fire. Then they settled down in the boma and waited. At ten o'clock a weasel appeared. At eleven, something a little larger, a hedgehog.

'I thought we were going to have a lot of company,' Roger said.

'I see a good deal of movement behind the bushes,' Hal said. 'Evidently there are quite a few animals but they are afraid to come out. Keep very quiet.'

Since the fire was not doing them any harm, the creatures of the forest began to appear. A couple of wolves came out, looking about suspiciously, and sat down where they could get the warmth of the fire.

Then came a Gir lion. Most other animals were afraid of him, so he expected this strange bright thing would also fear him. He walked straight up to it, growling, and expected the bright thing to run away. It did not run. He pushed his way into it and the fire caught in his whiskers. In great surprise, he backed off and rolled about on the ground to put out the blaze in his beard and his mane.

The boys saw a leopard hiding behind the bushes. He always took care not to be seen so he did not venture farther.

A sambar, and his friend a chital, came out together and these two fine deer joined the lion and the leopard.

At twelve, the most important guest appeared on the scene. He came galumphing in, pounding the

earth with his enormous flat feet. He was screaming like a steam whistle. The other animals ran for their lives from the rogue elephant.

One black cat of some sort ran up the tree and took refuge in the branches.

The rogue, trumpeting loudly, flung up his trunk, and danced the strange little two-step that all elephants do when about to attack. To him, the fire was a living thing and therefore to be killed. He rushed into it, stamped about on the embers, raging and squealing. But the fire won the contest. He ran out with scorched legs and made for the leopard behind the screen of bushes.

The leopard, instead of running away in a panic, took a flying leap and landed on the rogue's back. He dug in his long sharp claws and sank his teeth into the elephant's neck.

The elephant with a scream of pain and rage whirled his trunk about and knocked the leopard from his back.

Then the monster noticed the boma. He came at full speed and plunged his trunk and head into the thorns. His very sensitive trunk was pierced in many places. He was furious. If he charged again, down would go the boma and also two young hunters. He crashed once more against the boma and down it fell.

But the boys were no longer in the boma. They were at the base of the tree with the chain in their hands. Like lightning, the chain was flung around the tree and one of the legs and locked fast.

Now the song of the rogue could be heard for many miles. It so terrified the cat in the shaking

tree that it fell from a branch into the boma. Hal pushed it into the cage. He played his torch on it.

'It's a panther. What a lucky catch!'

'What's a panther?' Roger wanted to know.

'It's one of the leopard family. But it looks quite different. It's as black as coal. So they give it another name — panther. In a way it's better than a spotted leopard, because it's so unusual. Dad will be glad to have it.'

The villagers were streaming out to see what was going on. They saw their tormentor who had destroyed their crops, smashed houses, killed neighbours, now safely put out of business. The rogue was still dancing and trumpeting, but the tree, although shaking, did not come down.

Hal and Roger were glad to go to their cabin and get some sleep.

In the morning, Roger said, 'You can't leave him

there. What are you going to do with him? Why not shoot him?'

'That's not necessary,' Hal said. 'He's a very big, strong, powerful animal. He ought to be of great use to somebody after he gets over these tantrums. I'm going to see Abu Singh.'

'Who's Abu Singh?'

'Don't you remember — the Abu Singh Teak Company?'

'They couldn't make use of a crazy beast like that.'

'I'm not so sure,' said Hal. 'We'll see what Abu Singh thinks about it.'

At the timber-yard they met Abu Singh himself.

'We have a rampaging rogue elephant chained outside the village of Bahru. We can't do anything with him but perhaps you can.'

'What's the matter with him?'

'It's a case of musth,' Hal said. 'He's no use to you the way he is now, but in about a week he may be all right. He looks very strong and healthy and perhaps you could train him to be a good logger. It won't cost you one rupee.'

Abu Singh thought it over. 'Well, I can't lose on a deal like that. I'll send a couple of our tame elephants. With one on each side of him, firmly locked together, he can't do much. We'll keep him chained up until he gets over his heebie-jeebies. But I don't understand why you don't keep him yourself. You are take-'em-alive men.'

'Yes,' Hal said, 'but we already have an elephant. One is enough.'

So the rogue was left with Abu Singh who notified

the boys two weeks later that the great animal was
piling logs as if he had done it all his life.

19
Wolf and Dogwolf

'Oh-oh-ah-ah-ah-oo-oo-oo-oo-WEE-WEE-Wee-Wee-oo-oo-oo-oo-ah-ah-oh-oh.'

The weird sound woke Roger.

'What in the world is that? Hal, wake up. Did you hear that? It sounded like a wolf. It started low, went away up to a scream — "WEE-WEE-WEE-WEE", then down again.'

'You're right,' said Hal. 'It was a wolf. Strange — because Indian wolves don't often howl.'

He was interrupted by another cry: 'Oh-oh-oh-ah-ah-ah-oo-oo-WOOF-WOOF-WOOF-ah-oo-oh-oh.'

'I can't understand it,' Hal said. 'Those WOOFS in the middle. Those are barks, not howls. The wolf doesn't bark. The middle was dog sound. The start and finish were wolf sounds. How do you explain that?'

'I don't,' said Roger. He was already out of bed and pulling on his clothes. Hal dressed hastily. They didn't stop for breakfast.

They hopped into the truck and took off in the direction of the howls and barks.

'If we don't hurry,' Hal said, 'we may lose them

because they don't stay long in one place. They can cover from twenty-five to forty miles in a day. They run very fast and hardly anything can beat them except a cheetah.

'A cheetah can do seventy miles an hour but soon tires. A wolf can run all day or all night. If they have found something to eat we may get there in time.'

'What do they eat?'

'Anything from a mouse to a deer. They have a great taste for rabbits and rats. In America they used to follow the herds of buffalo, feeding on the stragglers, the sick and the dead. They have been known to kill and eat horses. In Russia they have chased sleighs, not to kill the people in the sleighs, but to kill the horses.'

'You mean they don't kill people?'

'Almost never.'

'That's good,' Roger said. 'Perhaps they don't like the taste of us.'

'They are very intelligent. Quite as clever as a fox. They know that if they kill people they will be killed. But if there are enough wolves in the pack they may attack men. That's not likely here because I understand that there are seldom more than six or eight wolves in an Indian pack.'

'You say they travel a lot. Don't they have any home?'

'Yes, and they come back to it every once in a while. If there is a hollow log lying on the ground they use that as a home. Or they will dig a hole into the side of a hill and keep digging until it may be thirty feet long. At the end of it is their home, sweet home.'

'I think we must be getting close to them,' Roger said. 'Their howling seems to get louder all the time.'

Hal slowed the truck to make it as quiet as possible. They rounded a little hill and there was a pack of seven wolves. They stared at the truck, but did not run away.

Now the boys were to discover why one of these animals could both howl and bark.

They were all large beasts, about five feet long. They had thick, shaggy coats so that they could go up into the mountain snows without getting cold.

Hal said, 'You notice how short their ears are. Up in the mountains long ears would get frostbitten. So nature has given them short ears that are not so likely to freeze.

'What terrific jaws they have,' Roger said.

'They can kill almost anything with those jaws. They have forty-two big teeth, each one as strong as a rock.'

'Look at that one jump. He must have made sixteen feet in one bound. Why aren't they afraid of us?'

'They are very wise animals,' Hal said. 'They can see that we have no guns.'

'Look. One of them is trotting this way,' cried Roger.

This animal seemed glad to see human beings. He came very close. He whimpered as if he wanted to be petted. Roger took a chance. He reached down and stroked the shaggy neck of the animal.

Then out came the howl and right in the middle of it were the barks of a dog.

'This is the one,' exclaimed Hal, 'the one we heard woofing. It's not a wolf, and it's not a dog. One of its parents was a dog and the other was a wolf. We were asked to get a wolf. All right, we'll get a wolf — but we'll also take home this dogwolf. He's a curiosity that will bring a lot of people to the zoo.'

The animal that Hal had called a dogwolf leaped up on to the truck, walked up to the back of the seat and put its head in between the two boys.

'I think he's adopted us,' said Hal. 'That's the easiest catch we ever made. In fact, we didn't catch him, he caught us. What a friendly beast! We have the dogwolf, now we must get the wolf.'

With a skilful fling of the lasso Hal necked the largest and finest of the wolves. He and Roger both laid hold of the rope and drew the howling wolf to the back of the truck.

'I'll get him up on to the truck,' Roger said.

'You can't do that,' Hal said, 'he must weigh nearly two hundred pounds.'

Roger went back. He jerked on the rope until the wolf angrily leaped up on the truck, snarling, ready to punish this boy for annoying him.

But Roger was no longer there. He was standing behind the cage, the door of which stood open. The animal was not used to cages. What he wanted was to get at the boy whom he could see plainly through the back of the cage. He walked in. Roger slipped round and closed the cage door.

Captured — one wolf. The dogwolf did not need to be captured. Evidently he had not seen human beings for a long time and he elected to stay with them. He didn't need to be caged. The dog in him trusted a dog's best friend — man.

So, wolf and dogwolf travelled back to camp. The wolf was caged. But the dogwolf ran free. He could be relied upon to stick around where he was petted, well fed, and safe.

At their long-delayed breakfast, Hal said, 'Roger, you remember reading *White Fang* by Jack London — about the animal called White Fang who was part dog, part wolf. And then there was that story by Kipling about the little boy called Mowgli who was brought up by a wolf. Since that was written there have been more stories about children being brought up by wolves. They are very common in India. One of these stories is about a small boy who had been abandoned at birth but was cared for by the wolves. He walked on his hands and feet, he could not speak any language, but he could howl like a wolf. Of course it was just a story, but many people believed it. Anyhow, such stories show that some people trust wolves and find there is much good in them. But I think the best qualities of all come out when you put dog and wolf together as you see them in our new friend, Dogwolf.'

20
The Houseboat

Hal had been working very hard collecting animals. He was very tired, almost sick. He needed a rest.

'You look like a ghost,' Roger said. 'Why don't you let up for a little while?'

'I've been thinking about doing just that,' Hal said. 'How would you like to go to the Vale of Kashmir for a week or two? It's just one of the loveliest places on earth.'

'That would be great,' said Roger. 'I've heard about it. Vale means valley, doesn't it? They have houseboats. Perhaps we could rent one and live on it. But who would take care of our animals?'

'That's the trouble,' admitted Hal. 'They would have to be fed every day, and they would have to be protected against crooks like those three in the barn-house. We'll have to find someone to take care of them. Suppose I go and see Abu Singh. We've given him an elephant worth millions of rupees. Perhaps he would be willing to do something for us.'

Hal found Abu Singh eating his breakfast. Abu Singh was happy to see him. 'Come, my good friend, sit down and eat with me.'

'Thank you, but I've already had breakfast,' Hal said.

'You look as if you needed more. Either that or rest. You are doing very hard work — why don't you relax for a little while?'

'I've been thinking about it. But someone will have to look after our animals. They would have to be fed. And it would be necessary to protect them against thieves who are very anxious to steal them.'

'Why don't you let me help?' said Abu Singh. 'I can't stay there myself, but I could have one of our men posted there.'

'Very kind of you,' Hal said. 'But he would have to be on the job day and night. He could use our cabin.'

'It will be a pleasure to do this for you,' said Abu Singh. 'You have done so much for me. The elephant you gave me is one of our best.'

He went to the door and called in a mahout. He said to Hal, 'This mahout's name is Akbar. Akbar, this is Hal Hunt who has a permit to collect animals in the Gir Forest. He has already made a fine collection. But it is very hard work and he and his brother are going away for a week or two. While they are away, I want you to look after their animals, feed them, and don't let anybody steal them. You may use their cabin. Can I rely upon you?'

'Certainly, Master. When shall I begin?'

'At once. Go back with Mr. Hunt and he will tell you just what each animal requires in the way of food.'

Hal liked Akbar and felt the job was in good

144

hands. He and Roger were free to go, and they left at once for New Delhi where they could get a plane for the wonderful valley of Kashmir.

The plane climbed to a dizzy height, passed through a narrow gorge, and came down to the most beautiful spot they had ever seen.

The valley was a cradle surrounded completely by Himalayan peaks. The river Jhelum ran through it and there were dozens of lakes. All the land was so green that it looked as if it had been painted yesterday. The plains below were hot, but here the air was delightfully cool. When the British governed India they would come every summer to Kashmir to get away from the terrific heat of the plains. They would live on houseboats. Now the British were gone but the houseboats were still there, three hundred of them lined up ready for use.

After landing, the boys inspected the houseboats. They picked one name *Lone Star*. At their request, it was poled across Dal Lake to a quiet little cove where it came to rest in a great bed of lotus. These magnificent plants have leaves as big as umbrellas and flowers of great beauty.

The boys felt they were in a sort of heaven. This was a hidden paradise which, once seen, could never be forgotten. Hundreds of years ago the emperors of India had made this their summer home. One of them, the Emperor Jahangir, had written:

Kashmir is a garden of eternal spring. Its pleasant meadows and enchanting cascades are beyond all description. There are running streams and fountains beyond count. Wherever the eye reaches there is running water. In the enchanting spring the hills and plains are filled with blossoms.

The great Himalayas crowned with snow and gleaming with glaciers completely encircle the valley. The lively green of growing things with the silver threads of streams, canals and lakes turn the whole into a sort of Himalayan Venice. The broad Jhelum River passes through lovely lake after lake on its way to join the mighty Indus.

The mountains are the world's highest. Nothing in the range stands at less than eighteen thousand feet. One soars to twenty-six thousand, another twenty-eight thousand while Everest tops the entire planet at twenty-nine thousand feet. Even the Vale of Kashmir itself is a mile high.

On a peak above the houseboat was a storybook castle, on another peak the maharajah's palace, and on another an ancient fortress.

'Let's take a look at our floating house,' Hal said.

In a hotel they would have one room. Here they had seven rooms. All beautifully furnished. The ceilings were of fine wood. The windows were large affording a wonderful view, the carpets were thick, and the bulging lamps were made of camels' stomachs. A stairway led up to the flat roof which was a hundred feet long, a fine place to stroll or sit and admire the beauty on every side.

'No better place than this in the world to rest,' Hal said.

One would not expect electric lights on a houseboat, electric fans, two baths, a well-stocked library, hand-carved furniture and oil paintings. But this floating palace had all that and more.

It did not have a kitchen. This was a blessing because there were no fumes from cooking stoves. Thirty feet behind the houseboat was the 'kitchen boat' where all the cooking was done and where the help lived. At mealtimes a butler came from the kitchen boat bearing trays of food which were unloaded on to the table in the dining-room and the butler stayed to serve the two lucky travellers.

And even that was not all. The houseboat itself did not move, but moored to its bow was a *shikara* or pleasure boat forty-five feet long, manned by four paddlers who would take you anywhere at any time of the day or night. You could take a trip by moonlight at two a.m. if you wished.

'Something like the gondolas they have in Venice,' Hal said, 'but a lot better. Instead of sitting upright you lie on those cushions. You have cushions under your back, cushions beside you, cushions under your head and cushions under your feet. There's a canopy above you and curtains that may be drawn against sun or wind. Let's go for a ride.'

No sooner said than done. They stepped into the shikara, nodded to the smiling boatman, waved a hand to indicate that they wanted to go round the lake, and off they went in a boat that was named *Abode of Peace.*

The shikara brushed through beds of lotus with their gorgeous pink-and-white flowers and three-foot leaves, through squat, contented water lilies and tall, swaying reeds as graceful as young girls, under a sky so clear it seemed no sky at all, and over open stretches of water so smooth that they seemed to consist merely of mountains upside down. One man sang softly to the accompaniment of a stringed instrument called a *sarangi*.

'Who knows what emperors have sailed in this boat,' said Roger. 'I feel like an emperor myself.'

The air was so clean that objects at a great distance seemed to be close by. It was as if they were looking at everything through a magnifying glass. There was good health in the breeze, no pollution anywhere. No wonder many Kashmiri lived to be a hundred.

Other shikaras drifted by, their names neatly displayed: *Dancing Girl, Spring Rose, Kashmir Glory, Rock and Roll.*

When the sarangist finished his song, there was no sound but the dip of paddles and the swoop of orange-breasted blue-backed kingfishers.

No roar of motors. A lake with no speedboats churning up the surface, destroying the mirror that held so many mountains.

'Look at the gardens!' exclaimed Roger.

They were not vegetable gardens, and they were not flower gardens although there were many flowers. They were lovely parks that had been established by the emperors of past ages. They covered miles along the shore. Great chinar trees as mighty and as old as the huge *sequoia gigantea* of California raised their heads almost two hundred feet high. Between them were dozens of streams, waterfalls and fountains. The shikara glided by the 'Garden of Breeze' laid out by the Emperor Akbar, the 'Garden of Pleasure' with its fountains falling over ten terraces, and the 'Royal Spring' designed by the Emperor Shah Jehan, creator of the Taj Mahal which is said to be the most beautiful building in the world.

In such a paradise the boys got back their strength. After a week they hired a car and drove up to Leh at an altitude of nearly twelve thousand feet.

Here they had none of the pleasant climate of the Vale. The thin, dry air could not resist the sun or hold the heat after the sun was gone. The temperature climbed to 120°F at noon and sank to 40°F at midnight.

The people of Leh got their living from herds of tough cattle and yaks. They could grow crops of barley and rice. They knew the ways of the otter and the antelope, the ibex and the Himalayan black bear, the gazelle, chital, musk deer, leopard, fox, jackal, wolf, wildcat and the handsome and graceful snow leopard.

The boys were sorry they had no way to transport some of these animals to their camp in the Gir Forest. But their chance would come later in the mountains above the Gir.

The boys came back to Kashmir and then travelled to Swat. This was a very small country surrounded by Pakistan which now governs its affairs.

But not so long ago it was a kingdom under the Ahkoond of King of Swat. The name 'Swat' is so curious that the playful poet, Edward Lear, wrote this jingle:

Who, or why, or which, or what
  Is the Akond of Swat?
Is he tall or short, or dark or fair?
Does he sit on a stool or sofa or chair,
  or SQUAT?

The land of Swat is about a hundred miles long
and fifty wide. It is watered by the Swat River. Its
half-million Swatis speak the Swat language. Everything is Swat in Swat.

Edward Lear was answered by another poet:

What, what, what,
What's the news from Swat?
      Sad news,
      Bad news,
Comes by cable led
Through the Indian Ocean's bed.
Through the Persian Gulf, the Red
Sea and the Med—
Iterranean — he's dead;
The Ahkoond is dead!

The boys stayed in the Swat Hotel and they dined
on Swat's chief export, honey. And they saw the
Swat dungeon where criminals were confined.

Next door to Swat the Hunts found another tiny
country, called Dir.

'Dir me,' said Hal. 'This is worse than Swat. No
schools, no colleges, no hospitals, except one for
dogs.'

The Prince of Dir kept forty dogs and forty wives.
Some of the Diris were pirates. If the border was

not carefully watched, a Swati cow would be carried off, or a Swati wife.

On the Hunts went to New Delhi and then to the Gir Forest and their precious animals which the mahout had cared for so well. In fact, he had added one more. It was a beautiful black-and-white giant panda, a visitor from nearby China, cousin of the red panda they had already captured.

'Good to be home,' said Hal, 'and good that not one animal has been stolen.' He tried to press some rupees upon Akbar but the mahout would not accept any payment.

'You have already paid us,' he said, 'a hundred times over. Your elephant is a great logger. Any time we can help you, let us know.'

21
Roger's Wild Buffalo

Walking in the forest, the Hunts suddenly came upon a herd of some thirty wild water-buffalo, the biggest and most dangerous of all oxen next to the gaur.

These great animals, weighing more than two thousand pounds, faced about and regarded the boys with angry tosses of their heads and deep bellows that told the newcomers that they were not welcome.

'Better get up a tree,' Hal said.

Roger lost no time in climbing a great pipal just as the biggest animal, which seemed to be the leader of the herd, came plunging towards him. The bad-tempered animal stopped below the branch occupied by Roger and tried to reach him with one of its long horns.

One would think that a creature weighing more than two thousand pounds would not be a very good dancer. But the angry beast gave a good demonstration of the polka, the waltz, and the tango, and even stood on its hind feet trying to get one of its sharp horns into its enemy.

'We've got to get him for Dad,' Roger shouted.

'Yes, she's just what he wanted.'

'What do you mean — she? No lady would ever act this way,' declared Roger.

'Perhaps you don't know much about ladies,' Hal said. 'They can be pretty tough sometimes. This lady would finish you off in a minute if she could reach you.'

'I can't stay here all day,' Roger said. 'What am I going to do?'

'Stay there all day,' Hal suggested. 'I don't think your friend has any intention of leaving. She's too fond of you.'

'Why does she pick on me? Why doesn't she chase you?' Roger wanted to know.

'Because I'm standing still. She probably thinks I'm just one of the trees. Water-buffaloes do not have very good eyesight. But they have a marvellous sense of smell. Perhaps you smell so good that she simply can't resist you.'

'You can joke,' Roger said, 'but it's no joking

matter if I have to stay here all day and perhaps all night.'

But the lady buffalo had no intention of waiting so long to get her horns into this trouble-maker. She couldn't reach him, so she tried something else. She would shake him out of the tree.

She backed off, then came at a run and threw every ounce of her tremendous weight against the trunk of the tree. The pipal shivered and shook and Roger fell.

But he did not fall to the ground. Instead, he found himself on the lady's back. The back was so broad that he could hardly straddle it. But he clung on and away went beast and boy to an unknown destination. Hal tried to keep up. He could just do it, because an animal so heavy could not make great speed.

The whole forest was excited by the race. The bird called the whistling schoolboy whistled his very loudest tune. The plover screamed something that sounded like 'Did-you-do-it? Did-you-do-it?' The monkeys screeched to high heaven. It was a great day for monkeys. They had never seen anything like this.

Hal managed to get the lasso over one horn but he could not stop the animal's wild rush. Instead, he lost his footing, fell down, and was dragged along like a sack of meal.

The plover seemed to be laughing. 'Did-you-do-it?' The bird was making fun of the boys. If anything was 'doing it' it was the gigantic beast, not the Hunts. The whistling schoolboy seemed to get a laugh into his whistling.

They arrived at a mudhole. Buffaloes love mud-holes. The muddier the better. The muddy water cools them on a hot day. They come out covered with mud which is just what the doctor ordered to keep off biting insects.

So down into the mudhole went the beast and its rider. It was deep enough so that the muddy water came up to Roger's neck and the animal was completely covered except for the eyes and nose.

Now here was a place where the buffalo was content to stay all day. Roger was thoroughly soaked and completely muddied. He would be a pretty sight when he came out — if he ever came out. The birds and monkeys found the whole show very entertaining.

A great osprey, or fish-eating hawk, came down from its enormous nest as wide as a car in the top of a tree to get a better look. Then its sharp eyes made out something that was even more interesting, a fish in the nearby river. It dropped like a stone into the river, dived deep, and came up with the fish in its beak. This was better than a boy in a mudhole. Quite satisfied with itself, it flew up towards its nest. It did not get there. An eagle swooped in from nowhere, seized the fish, and carried it off, perhaps to feed its baby eaglets.

Wasps began to buzz about the two heads, Roger's and the buffalo's. The buffalo solved her problem by sinking her entire head into the muddy pool. She held it there until the wasps gave up and centred their attention on the other head. To avoid being bitten, Roger took a lesson from the buffalo and buried his own head. When he could hold his breath no longer, he raised his head and was pleased to notice that the wasps had gone. He would not have been so pleased if he could have seen his own head and face plastered with mud.

Hal laughed. 'You look like someone who's just been dug up out of the grave. Where, oh where has my beautiful brother gone?'

'Stop your kidding,' Roger said. 'You ought to be thinking about how we're going to get out of this. I think I have an idea. I don't know whether it will work or not — but we might try it.'

'Well, what's the bright idea?'

'I didn't say it was bright — but it's better than nothing. You have one horn noosed. Give me the other end of the rope and I'll tie it on to the other horn.'

'Whatever for? Have you gone out of your head completely?'

'Perhaps,' admitted Roger. 'But give me the rope end and we'll see what we can do with it.'

He tied the rope to the horn. He drew it tight. The rest of the rope was in the boy's hands.

'What in the world are you up to?' exclaimed Hal.

Roger explained. 'If my lady and I ever get out of here, how are we going to get to camp? We can't expect Her Ladyship to go straight there and walk into a cage. She could go in any one of a hundred directions. I think I have the answer. I have what amounts to two reins in my hands. By pulling on the left one, I can turn her head left. By pulling on the right one I can pull her head right.'

'What makes you think she will turn her head either way?'

'I couldn't do it if the horns were short. But a very long horn gives me a lot of leverage. I think it will work, but I don't guarantee it.'

'Okay,' said Hal, 'when do we start on this horn-pulling trip to camp?'

Roger said, 'If you will give my fat friend a few good pokes with a stick behind, she may climb out of here and perhaps I can steer her to camp.'

'I think you're loony,' said Hal, but he got a sharp stick and began prodding the animal's rear. Since she was not so comfortable as she had been, she began to think of leaving the precious mudhole. A few more prods, and the buffalo struggled up out of the mudhole. She was beautifully plastered with mud from head to foot.

Hal laughed. 'She looks as bad as you do,' he said.

The lady started off in exactly the wrong direction. Roger pulled the rope attached to the left horn. That turned the animal's head to the left and she kept going farther left until she was headed straight towards camp. Then Roger stopped pulling, but whenever the great beast began to change direction he could bring her back by a gentle tug to the left or right.

It was necessary to cross the river to reach home. There was a bridge, but whether it could bear up under a ton of meat and bone, who could say? The lady started when she saw it. Perhaps she knew better than the boy on her back whether or not the bridge would hold her up. She tried hard to go to the right or the left along the bank. But her driver was determined to make her take the bridge.

So she took the bridge and when she reached the middle of it the bridge broke down and the buffalo and its rider got a bath that they had not asked for.

But, after all, the plunge into the clean river washed away two or three layers of mud. For this the boy was grateful. Clambering up on the other bank they proceeded, with some horn-jerking, towards the camp. Hal crossed by another bridge.

The buffalo was moving slowly now, probably thinking back to that lovely mudhole.

'Run ahead,' said Roger, 'and open a cage. Perhaps I can horn her right into it.'

It was done exactly as Roger had planned. The buffalo was steered into the cage. Roger slid down from her back and came out, closing the door.

'Well,' said Hal, 'I guess you're a little cleverer than I thought you were.'

'Thank you, my dear sir,' said Roger, 'for that lovely compliment. After this, anything you want to know about handling wild animals, just ask me.'

They both laughed, and at once started digging up great armfuls of long grass and stuffing them into the cage for a very hungry Madam Buffalo.

Roger noticed that the pile of grass went down the animal's gullet very speedily. He said, 'She'll get a stomach-ache if she eats so fast.'

'No,' said Hal. 'She's equipped with two stomachs. The food is chewed and then goes down into the first stomach where it is softened by certain gastric juices. Then it comes back up into the mouth for another chewing, after which it goes down into the second stomach and is digested. It's a very clever arrangement. We would do much better ourselves if we had two stomachs.'

Roger changed his clothes. Then Hal said, 'Now, how about our own dinner? You've been wanting some milk to drink.'

'I don't suppose there's any milk within a hundred miles,' said Roger.

'There's plenty of milk within a hundred feet,' said Hal. He got a pan and went into the buffalo's cage. The boys enjoyed the first milk they had had in many a day. It was so rich it seemed like cream.

'No Mr Buffalo could have given us that,' said Hal. 'I'm glad we got a Mrs'

22
Saved by a Monkey

Exploring the Gir Forest, Hal and Roger were suddenly stopped by a shrill cry. It was something like 'Na-na' and then a 'Whoomp-whoomp'. They looked up. There it was in the top of the tree. It looked as golden as the golden cats.

'What is it?' asked Roger.

'That's an animal that is not in any zoo in the world. It's a golden langur, a monkey that warns that there is danger. The zoo knows nothing about the golden langur. It was discovered recently by Dr. Gee, a famous naturalist.'

Again the langur called, 'Na-na. Whoomp-whoomp-whoomp.'

'Look where he's looking,' said Hal. 'There must be something dangerous there. Perhaps a tiger. The meat of the langur is delicious food for all the carnivores. So the langurs appoint a watchman to stay in a high tree and watch for enemies. This is the watchman, and he is warning his tribe and also warning us. But I don't see any sign of a tiger or anything else.'

'I do!' exclaimed Roger. 'See? It's a leopard.

There it goes, right up the same tree. It's going to kill that watchman.'

But the golden langur saw the spotted cat approaching, and with a great leap such as only a monkey can make, he jumped into another tree and came down to the ground. Then he ran to the boys and squeezed in between them.

'I do believe he wants us to protect him,' said Roger. 'He seems to take it for granted that we are his friends.'

'That is easily explained,' said Hal. 'The people of India are friends of the monkeys. They never kill them. The city of Calcutta swarms with monkeys. They get into all sorts of mischief but they are as sacred as the sacred cows and no one interferes with them.'

The leopard came down and ran off into the woods. He was not bold enough to attack two humans and a golden langur.

Hal pulled out his pocket camera. 'I want a picture of this animal,' he said. 'He's the most beautiful monkey I've ever seen.'

He backed off about ten feet and focused on the animals. When he was ready to shoot, the golden langur had disappeared.

Hal looked up and saw his langur and once more focused. Again when he was ready to shoot there was no langur. The third time he discovered what was the matter. The langur didn't wait to have his picture taken. Each time he took a flying leap behind Hal and peered down into the camera. What a charming and friendly animal, but so difficult to photograph!

They went home, Hal carrying the golden langur. On the way they met Vic. He also was carrying something — a weasel.

'I got this for you,' he said. 'It's going to cost you fifty dollars.'

Hal did not want a weasel, but he had promised to pay Vic fifty dollars for any animal he brought in. So he pulled out his wallet.

A weasel is hard to hang on to. This little fellow slid through Vic's fingers, leaped to the ground and disappeared.

For some strange reason Vic seemed to think he still deserved fifty dollars.

'I got it for you,' he said, 'and you have to pay me.'

'I'll pay you when I see it in a cage,' Hal said. 'I can't pay you for what I don't get.'

'But I got it,' whined Vic. 'It wasn't my fault that it escaped.'

'No,' said Hal, 'you just couldn't hang on to it. I don't pay you for what you can't deliver.'

Vic was not satisfied. 'You're a cheat,' he said. 'I'll get back at you for this. You can't swindle me and get away with it.' And he indignantly strode off to his barn-house.

'What a nasty guy,' said Roger. 'Never thanks you for what you do for him. Thinks he has a right to be paid for nothing. You'd better watch out. Right now I'll bet he's thinking up some mean trick he can play on you.'

Reaching camp, they put the golden monkey in a cage and were sorry that the cage itself was not golden because this remarkable animal deserved the best.

'I wonder if he's had his lunch,' Roger said.

'A watchman doesn't eat anything while he's on duty. He watches every moment for enemies. So he's probably very hungry.'

'What sort of food does he eat?'

'Leaves, grass, caterpillars, insects, fruits and berries, spiders, tarantulas, cockroaches, anything that grows and anything that crawls.'

So Roger proceeded to collect leaves, fruits, caterpillars, insects, spiders, tarantulas, worms, small birds, scorpions and other such delicacies, all of which were heartily appreciated and gobbled down by the beautiful guest. Goldie thanked Roger with a 'Whoomp-whoomp' and a 'Ha-ha'.

'And he'd like salty earth if you can find some.'

Roger found a salt lick and collected plenty of the dirt. The golden langur enjoyed this lovely dessert.

In the middle of the night Goldie set off his alarm, a loud 'Whoomp-whoomp-whoomp-na-na-na'.

'The watchman is warning us,' said Hal. 'Something is wrong.'

Pyjama-clad, they rushed out to find Vic setting fire to the cabin. Roger doused the flame with a pail of water while Hal grabbed Vic and tossed him into the river. Vic climbed out, soaking wet. He started for the barn-house, hurling back threats as to what he was going to do to the Hunts. 'It'll be worse next time,' he promised them.

The boys went to thank Goldie. Without his warning their cabin would now be a pile of ashes. Roger put his fingers in through the wires of the cage. Goldie licked them, and an eternal friendship was sealed between the Hunts and the beautiful golden langur who had saved them from disaster.

23
Hal's Sloth Bear

'Who's he? I've never seen him around,' Hal said.

The man they saw down the path ahead of them was certainly very strange. Although it was a hot day, he was dressed in a fur coat that came down to his feet. It even went up over his head like a hood. It covered his ears, his forehead, and his chin. Only his eyes and his long snout could be seen.

'He must be a madman to cover himself so completely on such a hot day.'

He stood almost six feet tall. He must have had poor eyesight and poor hearing because he did not appear to notice the boys or to hear them. The Hunts concealed themselves behind some bushes and watched.

The man in the big black overcoat was doing something very strange. He stuck out his tongue, and what a tongue it was, at least a foot long. Beside him was a termite hill and he stuck his tongue deep into it, got it covered with the little creatures that looked like ants, but were white, then brought his tongue back into his mouth and swallowed a breakfast of termites.

No man in his senses would eat live termites, and no man, whether in his senses or not, would have so long a tongue.

'It's not a man,' Hal said. 'It's a sloth bear. What looks like a fur coat is its long black hair.'

'But no bear could stand up so long on its hind feet,' Roger said.

'This bear can.'

'Is it really a bear? It looks more like a bad dream.'

Hal said, 'You've asked a good question — is it really a bear? The naturalists who name animals had a hard time naming this one. That long tongue business makes it look more like an ant-eater. But it's certainly no ant-eater, so they decided to call it a bear.'

'But you said it was a sloth bear. Why the sloth?'

'Because it is as slow as the sloth — but it can move at great speed if it is bent on killing a man or beast. It's one of the most dangerous of animals. Of course the sloth is very different. You've seen them in the tropics hanging upside down from a branch and hardly moving all day. The sloth bear stands up on its hind feet when it pleases and is always ready to wrestle with anyone who comes within reach.'

'Are there any sloths in the Gir Forest?'

'Not a single one. They belong in the American tropics.'

'But I never heard of such a thing as a sloth bear,' Roger said, 'till Dad wanted us to get one. How did he know about it? Does any zoo have a sloth bear?'

'I've never seen one in a zoo. Hardly anybody knows about it. But your father is pretty clever, and somehow or other he knew that there were sloth bears in the Gir Forest. And now it's up to us to get this one.'

Roger didn't think that would be hard. 'If it has only a tongue in its mouth it can't be very dangerous.'

'It doesn't fight with its tongue,' said Hal. 'At this distance you can't see its claws. They are terrible curved scimitars four inches long. They are as sharp as spears and could scratch the life out of you in two minutes.'

'Then how can we take him? Did you bring your sleep-gun?'

Hal said, 'No, but I have this.' He drew out of his pocket a slingshot. Between the two prongs was a strip of rubber cut from an old tyre.

'He's coming this way,' Roger exclaimed.

Hal picked up a stone and fitted it into the rubber strip. When the beast, still erect, came within twenty feet, Hal fired. The stone struck the animal's head with such force that he would have staggered and fallen if Hal had not leaped out and held him up.

'Quick!' Hal said. 'While he's so dizzy that he doesn't know what's happening, we'll walk him home and put him in a cage.'

Luckily, home was near by and the woozy bear was in the cage before his brain got over the shock. Then the ant-eater/bear went wild. With his terrible claws he attacked the bars that held him in. He let out sharp, gargling cries. He was capable of many sound effects. He screamed, he woof-woofed, he made a buzzing sound like a swarm of bees. He inflated his chest like a bagpipe and made bagpipe noises. Finally his voice died down to a grumbling, rumbling and mumbling.

Hal threw into the cage some wild sugar-cane, also a quart bag of the purple grape-like berries of the jumlum tree that he had gathered for his own lunch.

These foods are so highly esteemed by sloth bears that this animal changed his mind at once about his cage. It was a fine residence for him, he thought, if he could get food like this without any effort.

'They are said to be very intelligent,' Hal said. 'They actually know when to go to certain trees for ripe fruit, for the boram berry in one month, the mango in another, the jumlum berries exactly when they are at their best, and other foods when they are in season. They become tame, and even affectionate. Very few zoos have discovered the sloth bear and any zoo would be happy to get this unique gentleman in his black overcoat.'

24
Up, Up, Up

'I think it's about time for us to close in on those Hunts,' Vic said to Jim and Harry. 'Don't forget, you promised to back me up. Some day when they are off hunting animals we'll get some men to help us and we'll take all their animals that they have collected to New Delhi and sell them to zoos in India, Burma, Singapore and Japan for thousands and thousands of dollars. How does that sound to you?'

'It sounds fine,' said Jim, 'if you can pull it off. You don't seem too good at pulling anything off. You could have earned fifty dollars for every animal you brought in, but the only thing you caught was a weasel and you let it get away.'

'Could I help that?' said Vic. 'It was slippery.'

'You're pretty slippery yourself. Your dad has given you up as a bad job. He's cut off your allowance and we've had to support you. When are you going to get down to business and earn your own way?'

'Right now,' Vic said. 'Give me some money and I'll go to New Delhi and hire a couple of dozen trucks. Then some day we'll hire some men from

171

the villages to help us and we'll pile everything, animals, cages and all, on the trucks, and roll away.'

Jim laughed. 'Do you suppose the Hunts will let you do that?'

'We'll do it, some day while they are off hunting animals.'

Jim and Harry reluctantly agreed to Vic's plan. They gave him the money he needed and he was off to New Delhi.

When he came back a few days later he reported success. 'I hired the trucks and they will be here tomorrow. Now I'm going to take a walk down and look at our animals.'

'They are not our animals yet,' said Jim, 'but at least we can all go down and take a look.'

They went to the Hunt camp. Nothing was there except the cabin and it was locked. There were no cages, no animals. No one was around except the headman of Bahru Village.

'What's happened?' Vic asked the headman.

'Didn't you know? They moved out two days ago. Sent everything to Bombay to be loaded on a freighter for New York.'

'So they are in Bombay?'

'No, they are going up the mountain to get a few more specimens. They mentioned a blue bear, a white tiger, a snow leopard and a yak.'

'Why didn't they keep their camp here until they got those extra animals?' Vic asked.

'Because they were afraid they would be stolen while they climbed the mountain. They said there are thieves about. I don't know who they meant.'

172

'But,' objected Jim, 'they have to have equipment for climbing a mountain — crampons, ice-axes, all sorts of things.'

'Yes,' said the headman, 'they will get them at the first village on the way up. The village of Aligar.'

'Well,' said Harry to Vic, 'that knocks all your plans into a cocked hat.'

'Not quite,' said Vic. 'I'm going to follow them. They can't get away from me so easily. Perhaps I can help them have an accident.' He was careful to whisper this so that the headman should not hear. 'Then I can help them out by taking charge of their animals — the white tiger, snow leopard, blue bear and all — they sound pretty good to me.'

The headman went off to his village, shaking his head. This talk about thieves. Who could the thieves be? That Vic Stone was a good fellow. He was going to help the Hunts. If they had an accident, he would take care of their animals. Very nice, to have a friend like that.

As for Jim and Harry, they had had enough. Their vision of great wealth had faded. They no longer aspired to be great hunters like Hemingway and Corbett. It wasn't worth the trouble. They decided to go to Bombay and try to stow away on a ship bound for New York. Vic was sorry that they had come to this decision — sorry, because he could not depend upon them for more money. He could expect nothing more from his father. Perhaps if he could get the Hunts into trouble and walk off with those very valuable animals he might be able to sell them for, say, ten or twenty thousand dollars. That wasn't as much as he had hoped for, but it was a tidy sum. In the meantime, Hal and Roger had driven their truck loaded with cages up to the village of Aligar at an altitude of ten thousand feet. Here they could buy supplies for the further climb up the mountain.

First they bought heavy woollen clothing since on the heights the temperature would be far below zero. They bought crampons — spikes to be strapped to the soles of their climbing boots that would give their feet a firm grip on snow or ice. They bought a rope ladder which could be hung from a steel spike and would make it possible to climb very steep rocks or glaciers. They bought pitons — metal spikes to be driven into rock or ice with a rope attached so that by climbing up the rope they could move straight up to a higher level. They bought dark goggles which would prevent 'snow blindness' due to the glare of the sun upon the snow. They rented a tent for themselves and another for the Sherpas, professional guides who would carry their supplies and lead them up the extremely dangerous slopes. And they bought a hundred feet of rope.

The shopkeeper told them. 'Look out for the Yeti. They are very bad this year.'

'What are the Yeti?' Hal asked.

'Your people call them the Abominable Snowmen. Our own name for them is Yeti.'

'That's a better name for them,' Hal said, 'very short and easy to say. Yeti.'

Roger added, 'That was one thing Dad wanted us to do — investigate the Abominable Snowman.'

174

The shopkeeper said, 'Many people who go up never come down again. They are killed by the Yeti. The Yeti eat them. We never find their bodies or their bones.'

'What is a Yeti?' Hal asked. 'A man or a beast?'

'No one knows. We don't know what they are like. They are invisible. If you see a Yeti, you die. Some say they are ten feet tall. Others say a Yeti is a monster ninety feet tall and forty feet through.'

'But do you have any proof that these monsters exist?' Hal asked.

'One was here last night,' said the shopkeeper. 'Come outside and I'll show you his footprints.'

The footprints in the snow seemed to have been made by a monster with feet at least five feet long.

'Come back into the store and I'll show you further proof.'

He took down from a shelf a great woolly thing and laid it on the counter. 'That's the scalp of a Yeti,' he said.

Looking at it made Roger's nerves creep. 'What a giant this Yeti must have been.'

'It's the only Yeti scalp I have left,' said the shopkeeper. 'Perhaps you would like to buy it.'

'How much?' asked Hal.

'Well, in your money — it would amount to a thousand dollars. Remember, it is unique. You will probably never see another like it.'

Hal thought he could get along without seeing another like it. 'I'm sorry,' he said, 'we didn't bring that much money with us. Someone else will have to be the lucky buyer.'

'I'm sorry too,' said the shopkeeper, 'You're losing the chance of a lifetime.'

At this moment Vic walked in. He was puffing hard after his climb, although the slope that he had climbed was nothing compared with what they would find later on.

The Hunts were not pleased. They thought they had put this crook behind them forever.

'I came to help you out,' said Vic. 'I knew you couldn't do this alone. It's a dangerous business — mountain climbing.'

'And I suppose you've had a great deal of experience in mountain climbing,' Hal said.

'I've climbed the hills around the town of Brecon, in Wales. And I've climbed the Catskills. By the way, that was a dirty trick you played on me.'

'What was the dirty trick this time?' said Hal.

'Sending all those animals away without consulting us.'

'What business was it of yours?'

'Merely that I could have helped you.'

'Yes,' said Hal, 'that was what we were afraid of.'

Vic pouted. 'Now that was a mean thing to say. But I forgive you. Anyhow, here I am, ready to be of service.'

'So good of you,' Hal said. 'But it's really not safe for you. They say the Yeti are very bad this year.'

'What are the Yeti?'

'Oh, just monsters that chew you up and spit you out if they don't like the taste of you.'

'Are you kidding me?'

'Ask anybody. They all know about the Yeti. Look

176

at the footprints in the snow just outside the door. A Yeti was here last night. And if you don't believe the footprints, look at this Yeti scalp. You can have it for a thousand dollars.'

'That reminds me,' said Vic. 'I have no money. You'll have to buy some gear for me. Of course I'll pay you back when my cheque comes.'

'You're quite aware that no cheque will come,' said Hal.

He couldn't help feeling sorry for this dunce. Somebody had to look after him. He could get nothing from his father. Hal resigned himself to the job of keeping an eye on this helpless fool.

'Well,' he said, 'you can go with us if you will really buckle down and help get the specimens we are after.'

'Now you're talking,' said Vic. 'I knew you couldn't get along without me.'

Hal turned to the shopkeeper. 'Fit him out with everything,' he said. 'I'll pay for it.'

This was done. Then the man behind the counter said, 'The mayor sends word he would like to see you. His house is the big one on the left as you go down the street.'

The mayor's house was made of mud with sticks embedded in it. The roof was covered with animal skins all sewn together to keep out the rain and snow.

The mayor was very cordial. 'How do you enjoy the Himalayas — the highest mountains in the world? You will have tea with me — is it not so?'

'That will please us very much,' said Hal.

Tea was brought. It was strange stuff, but Hal and

177

Roger drank it. Vic took one taste and that was all.

'You don't like it?' asked the mayor.

'It's rank,' said Vic. Politeness was not one of his charms.

Hal was admiring the mud walls. 'They are very good to keep out the cold,' he said. 'Boards would have cracks between them. These walls are all solid — not a breath of wind can get in through them. May I ask what you use on the roof?'

'It is made of animal skins, all stitched together — jackal, gazelle, blue bear, otter, musk deer, wildcat, and ibex.'

'For the love of Pete!' exclaimed Vic.

'I beg your pardon?' said the mayor. 'Who is this Pete?'

'Just a friend of his,' Hal said, trying to smooth things over.

Vic leaped up, screaming. He had been sitting on the ground since there were no chairs. He itched in a hundred places at once.

'Ah,' said the mayor, 'you have been sitting on my private ant-hill. We produce our own ants because there is nothing that gives a pudding a better taste than a few of those peppery ants. Just remove your clothes, my friend, and we shall remove the ants.'

There was nothing for it but Vic must take off all his clothes and the mayor personally picked off the ants that were feasting on the boy's soft flesh, and put them carefully in a bottle to be used to pep up the next meal.

'Now you see,' said the mayor, 'they did warm

178

you up a bit, didn't they? Even an ant has its virtues. We are Buddhists and believe that all things work together for good, even these humble little ants. By the way, I hope you have not come up the mountain to kill our animals.'

'Your men must have killed a lot of them to get enough skins to make a roof,' said Vic.

'No, my boy,' said the mayor, 'these skins are all from animals that have died in the snow.'

Hal said, 'You ask whether we are here to kill animals. We never kill animals — we take them alive for zoos in the United States and elsewhere. There they are well cared for and survive longer than they would in the wild where there are so many men with guns.'

'Excellent,' said the mayor. 'You are as good as a Buddhist. Would you like to see the monastery? Is it just over the hill.'

The boys went to the monastery. The lamas, or priests, received them cordially. Hal asked them about the Yeti. Did they believe in them or not?

'Of course we believe in them,' said the head lama. 'A few days ago at the time of evening prayer the Yeti came snuffling round the building and tried to enter through a window. We were all terrified. We clashed our ceremonial cymbals and they went howling away into the night sounding like humans in great pain.'

'Was that the only visit you have had by Yeti?' Hal asked.

'No, they came again recently. We were settling to sleep one night when we were startled by the sound of footsteps. We looked out the window and there was a Yeti with a head as large as a bush and two flaming eyes. Not one of us dared move or reach for a gun. Finally we blew the great copper horns and the Yeti disappeared. By the way, we have some very good relics of Yeti and will sell them if you care to have them.'

'Not just now, thank you,' said Hal. 'We wonder if you can put us up for the night? We leave early tomorrow morning to go up the mountain.'

'Make yourselves at home,' said the head lama, 'if you don't mind sleeping on the floor.'

25
Bats for Breakfast

The floor was hard, and they were glad to rise soon after dawn. The head lama was already up.

'Have you said your prayers?' he asked.

'No,' said Hal.

'You may use that wheel in the corner.'

How could you use a wheel for prayer?

'Perhaps you do not know how to pray with a wheel,' said the lama. 'Let me explain.'

He took them across the room to the prayer-wheel which was about a foot in diameter and was bracketed to the wall.

'Now this wheel is hollow. Inside it is a parchment on which are written one thousand prayers, each ten words long. All you have to do is turn the wheel once all the way round and you have offered up a thousand prayers. It's a great improvement on your Western way of saying only one prayer. It's a thousand times more effective. After you have made your prayers you will join us for breakfast. I think you will enjoy what we have for breakfast. It's something very special.'

The lama bowed and left the boys to say their prayers.

Hal turned the wheel all the way round.

'That's my thousand,' he said.

Roger did the same. Vic waited until the other two were not looking. He turned the wheel round twice. That gave him two thousand prayers. Perhaps this would give him good luck all day long.

Almost at once he had bad luck. Sitting down at the breakfast table, which was surrounded by all the lamas, Vic looked suspiciously at the food on the plate before him. It was as black as charcoal. It appeared to be meat of some kind, perhaps the meat of a chicken. That was all right — he liked chicken. He began to pick at it and was astonished to find that it was full of fine bones. No chicken he had ever eaten was so full of little bones.

'This must be a very unusual chicken,' he said as he began to eat.

'It is something rather better than chicken,' said the head lama.

'Well, it is very good,' Vic admitted.

'You know what it is, of course,' said the head lama. 'It is grilled bat.'

Vic could not believe his ears. 'Did you say — bat?'

'Yes,' said the lama proudly, 'the big bat, sometimes known as the flying fox because it looks so much like a fox with wings.'

Vic got up and stepped outdoors and they could hear him vomiting. The flying fox flew up through his gullet and out of his mouth. He came back looking weak and white. 'That's the most awful thing I ever had in my mouth,' he said. And a moment before he had said it was very good. That showed he was not shocked by the taste, but only by the word 'bat'. Other things were offered to him but he refused to eat any more. Hal and Roger ate the bat with gusto. It was really very good food. They judged foods by their taste, not by their names. They had eaten grasshoppers in India, python in Africa, raw fish in Japan, living oysters in America — so why not bat?

Surely no other animal was constructed as this one was. It had such a labyrinth of bones that it seemed to be made of bars, bolts and braces.

But when the dusky flesh was extracted and tasted it was eaten with good appetite. It really was a delicacy, rather gamy, more tender then chicken. Since the 'flying fox' eats nothing but fruit its flesh is very tasty.

The cook came in and was pleased that the boys enjoyed their breakfast.

'I'm glad you like it. I am sorry — we have it only once a week.'

Vic thought that was once too often.

Quite refreshed by their meal of bat meat, yak milk and coarse bread covered with yak butter, the boys were ready to go — except Vic, he of the empty stomach. Outside the door were the nine Sherpas they would take with them. They were loaded with all the equipment that Hal had bought, besides warm woollen blankets, small oil stoves to be used in the tents, and bottles of oxygen in case at high altitudes there was not enough oxygen in the air to supply the lungs. The Sherpas had also bought two sleds, each six feet wide.

'What are they for?' Hal asked.

The Sherpa leader replied, 'If you should want to bring down an animal much too heavy for us to carry, we shall need a sled.'

'You speak English well,' said Hal. 'Do all your men speak English?'

'They have to know some English because most of the foreigners who come to climb the mountain are British or American and their only language is English.'

So they started up the mountain in search of — wildlife. Vic complained that it was very cold. Temba, the chief Sherpa, said, 'The colder it is, the safer. All the loose rock is frozen solid by the cold. There is less chance of avalanches. The snow is hard enough to walk on. The snow bridges over crevasses are more likely to be solid. You'll be in more danger a little later in the morning when the snow begins to thaw.'

Vic wished he could be back in the monastery a little later in the morning. But there was no chance of that. He must go on.

He marvelled that these Sherpas should work for so little. The head lama had told the boys that the Sherpas worked for twenty-eight dollars a month. How could they live on that? Hal was paying them more but Temba objected. 'You're spoiling them,' he said.

The terrific wind was a problem. It lifted Vic off his feet and laid him down flat on a snowbank. Hal and Roger clung together and their combined weight kept them from blowing away. Only the Sherpas did not notice the wind.

They came to a glacier and without the spikes called crampons on their boots they would have slid all the way back to the village. Frequently they came to a crevasse, a deep crack in the glacier that might go down nearly a hundred feet. If you fell down into it, the shock of landing on the rocks below would probably kill you. In some places there was a bridge of snow over the crevasse, and you could take your life in your hands and try to cross it. Snow did not make a very good bridge. Likely as not it would give way when you were in the middle of it and down you would go. If you happened to be the last in the procession, as Vic usually was, nobody might notice that you had disappeared and you would starve to death or freeze to death with no hope of rescue.

Hal tried to keep an eye on Vic, but it was difficult to look back and walk forward without plunging into a snowbank or dropping into a crevasse.

The sun was hot now, and everything was melting. Vic saw a snow cave. There it would be cool. He stepped into it and expected to catch up with the others a little later.

Yes, it was cool here and he thought he was quite bright to take advantage of it. He was tired of walking. He had no food inside to hold him up. The coolness of this retreat was delicious. He told himself that the others were not as bright as he was. They had passed right by this pleasant cave.

The increasing heat had a natural effect upon the roof of the snow cave. Suddenly the entire roof fell and completely closed the entrance with a bank of snow perhaps five or six feet thick. Now everything was black inside the cave. Vic could see nothing. He lost his sense of direction. He began clawing with his fingers but he was not operating in the right place. Instead of pulling away the snow that barred the entrance, he was wasting his energy on the side of the cave where he could go a hundred feet or more without coming out into the light.

He had been clever to get into the cave, but was not clever enough to get out. He began to get hungry and thirsty. He stuffed snow into his mouth to allay the thirst but there was nothing he could do about hunger. Snow caves are not equipped with cupboards full of food. He wished that he had not been so squeamish about eating bat. Perhaps his refusal to eat would mean his death.

He began to whimper and weep. Men did not whimper and weep, but he was finding out that he was not quite a man. He was very much like a small boy who wanted his mother or an earthquake — but he had hastened his mother's death, and the earthquake that might have broken open the entrance to his prison did not choose to come at this moment.

Temba was the first to notice that the boy who had been lagging behind could no longer be seen.

'Sahib,' he said, 'where is your brother?'

'Right here beside me,' said Hal, indicating Roger.

'No. I mean your other brother.'

'Vic Stone? I'm glad to say he is not my brother.'

186

He looked back along the trail. There was no sign of Vic. 'Perhaps he has gone back to the village,' Hal said.

'No, I have seen him following us. I think he must have had an accident along the way.'

Hal was reluctant to waste time. 'I suppose we'll have to go back and see what happened.'

They went back, passed the cave, and continued for a mile.

'We must have gone by him,' said Temba. They retraced their steps and came to a place where snow and ice had fallen.

Roger said, 'That looks funny. It wasn't that way when we came by here first.'

His keen eyes saved Vic's life.

A shovel that had been brought along for just such accidents was put to work. After half an hour of digging, a hole was made big enough for a face, and the face that appeared was Vic's.

'I thought you'd never come,' he complained. 'What's the idea of leaving me in this hole and walking off without me?'

Temba was surprised by this rudeness but Hal told him, 'Don't mind him. That's just his way.'

Vic continued to rant and rail at those who had saved him while they dug deeply enough so that he could step out of his prison.

'I want to go back to the village,' Vic said.

'That's a very good idea,' said Hal. But Temba advised against it.

'He would just get lost,' he said. 'He'll have to go on with us.'

There was a sound back in the cave and it was

not the voice of Vic. Hal could see away back in the rear a bluish something that moved. It came lumbering out, growling. It was the right moment for Hal's sleep-gun. He shot one dart and then, because the monster was so large, he shot another. The animal stopped, raised a paw and rubbed it over the spot that had been touched by the darts. He gazed at the men as if wondering what to do next. Then he decided to lie down and think it over. In a few minutes he was fast asleep.

'Did you want a blue bear?' Temba asked.

'That was one of the animals we especially wanted,' said Hal.

'Well, you have it,' said Temba. 'And he's one of the finest blue bears I've ever seen.'

The bear was a big fellow, perhaps five hundred pounds and his coat was a beautiful blue and black combination that vaguely reminded Hal of the Yeti scalp that had been shown to him by the shopkeeper.

It took all the men to lift the heavy bear on to a sled and, without delay, the whole party returned to the village of Aligar and the great blue bear was stuffed into a cage.

When he woke he began to tear about wildly until some food was introduced and he settled down to eat.

As for Vic, he was still in a daze. He had trouble remembering what had happened. When he got back his senses and realised the awful truth that he had shared his cave with a blue bear — he fainted.

26
Hunting the Horrible Yeti

'There are several different kinds of Yeti,' said Temba, the head Sherpa, as they climbed the next day in a slightly different direction. 'One is a shaggy monster ten feet tall when he is standing up, but he often prefers to go on all four feet like a bear. These Yeti are very troublesome because they prey on our cattle. Then there is the man-eating Yeti with a head that rises to a point. The male has a long mane that hangs over its eyes. It goes about wailing and whistling until it finds a man, woman or child to eat. We never find the bones — evidently this Yeti has such powerful jaws that it can eat the bones as well as the flesh. Many of our friends have gone up into the mountain and have never returned. We think they were devoured by this Yeti.

'Then there is a very savage Yeti that can devour a whole party of men as easily as you would eat a dozen grapes.

'There's a giant Yeti twenty feet tall, very much like a man, covered with long hair. He looks like a gorilla. But he doesn't act like a gorilla. The gorilla will not eat men, but this Yeti likes nothing better.

'There's still another Yeti but much larger, with flaming eyes and teeth a yard long.

'And then there is the ninety-foot monster that must be the lord supreme of all Yeti.'

'Are there any female Yeti?' Hal asked.

'Yes. We call them Yetini. They are kind to our children, but they devour our cats, dogs and pigs.'

The boys kept looking about for a Yeti — and hoping they would see one.

Hal said, 'The shopkeeper told us that the Yeti are. invisible.'

'They would be invisible to the shopkeeper. But they can be seen by the lamas, and sometimes by good people like you. A lama in the next monastery saw one. He was awakened by the sound of heavy breathing and scratching and a very bad smell. He looked out of the open window and saw the Yeti. He offered up a very loud prayer and the Yeti shrank away. The next morning the footprints could be seen in the snow, like a man's footprints, but much larger.

'A Yeti can change its size — small one moment and big the next. One would shrink to the size of a beetle and not look a bit dangerous. He would watch for someone to come along, then in the twinkling of an eye he would become a giant ogre. He would seize the passer-by and eat him up, clothes, bones and all, and leave not a trace behind.

'Sometimes,' said the Sherpa, 'a Yeti is kind to a man. A certain lama lost in the mountains was fed

191

day after day by a Yeti. Then one day the lama realised that he had not been fed for several days. He went searching and found the Yeti dead in a cave.'

Vic was quaking with fear. He kept peering about. He took off his dark snow-glasses so he could see better. The sun reflecting on the snow was very painful and he at once replaced the snow-glasses on his nose.

'They wouldn't really attack us, would they?' he said.

'Oh, of course not,' said the Sherpa. 'They might push us over a cliff, make us fall into a crevasse, bury us in an avalanche, give us snow blindness, lock us in an ice cave, torture us with dizziness, and if you saw one you would die of fright.'

Hal had a suspicion that Temba was kidding. He saw that Vic was taking it all as gospel truth. Vic was as crazy with dread as if he were already in the long claws of a Yeti.

'Go easy,' Hal said to Temba. 'He's scared to death.'

Now they were all too busy to think about Yeti. From every side came the sound of running water. Under the hot sun snow was melting, causing hundreds of streams and cataracts and waterfalls. Some of the falls were so high that the water turned into mist before it completed its drop.

They could not avoid the streams. If they could not jump over them, they had to wade through. The streams were shallow, yet deep enough to reach above their boot-tops.

They came upon a group of animals having a

lot of fun sliding down the snow, then up over a snowdrift.

'What are they?' Roger asked.

'Otters,' said Hal.

'There couldn't be otters way up here at eleven thousand feet.'

Temba said, 'You'd be surprised. There are shrimp in these streams at fifteen thousand, spiders at seventeen thousand. Here at eleven thousand, we have birds, musk deer, wild dogs, blue sheep, wolves, bears, pandas, gazelles, antelopes and ibex — not to mention the Yeti. And I forgot to include the white tiger and the snow leopard.'

'Those are two that we want,' said Hal.

'Don't you want an otter?' Roger asked.

'I'm afraid not. These are river otters. And we couldn't very well take a river along with us. Besides, Dad didn't ask for an otter.'

'Why are they sliding down? Does it do any good?' Roger asked.

'They are just playing. They slide down, then go back and slide down again and repeat over and over.'

Vic said, 'Animals don't play. They are too busy hunting for food.'

'Not always,' Hal said. 'Many animals play just for the fun of it. Kittens play, dogs play, tiger cubs play, pandas play — a sense of humour is not limited to human beings.'

'Look at the baby getting a ride,' said Roger.

Sure enough — a baby otter, sitting on its mother's chest, was enjoying the snow slide. Down they came, then up over the snowbank, and down again. When they came to a stop the mother, who had been sliding on her back, turned over so she could scramble up again to the top of the slide. But she didn't lose the baby. Although upside down, the young one clung to its mother's fur and when they reached the top they at once took another slide. It was very plain that they were having a good time, and it had nothing to do with hunting for food.

'Of course otters do get hungry,' Hal said. 'The sea otter dives down to the floor of the ocean and picks up a couple of shellfish, then rises to the surface where it lies on its back with the shellfish on its chest. It breaks the shells by cracking them together, then eats the squirming things that are inside. When it can get only one shellfish it hunts around for a stone, then comes up and breaks the shell with the stone. I suppose these river otters behave in much the same way.'

'I didn't imagine we would see otters here,' Roger said.

'Wherever there is water you will find them all over the world, except in Australia.'

'How bright their eyes are, and look at their cute whiskers, and their shiny brown fur,' Roger said. 'And look at the broad webbed feet like paddle-wheels. I suppose that's what makes them good swimmers.'

'They can swim a quarter of a mile under water,' said Hal. 'Few animals can go as fast. They can cover six miles in an hour. They can stay underwater for four hours before they have to come up to breathe. They make affectionate pets but they must be handled with care because they can inflict a very serious bite.'

'Is their skin valuable?'

'A large furry skin costs a thousand dollars or more.'

'But suppose all lakes and rivers are frozen over, what do they do then?'

'They spend most of their time in their burrow which may be twenty feet or more long. If the ice on a lake is not too thick they break it with a stone and swim down after fish or shellfish. If a man has a tame otter he can train it to do his fishing for him. The otter will bring up a fish between his forepaws and deliver it to his master without taking a bite. When the man has enough fish he will give back one or two so that the otter can have a reward for his good work.'

The otters, having finished their game, disappeared.

Roger said, 'I think I'll take a trip down that slide and see if it's as much fun as the otters think it is.'

Down he came like the wind, shot up over the snowbank and down the other side.

'It's great,' he said to Vic. 'Why don't you try it?'

'That's just child's play,' Vic said. 'Anybody can do that.'

'All right — go ahead and do it.'

'I can't be bothered. I don't play kids' games.'

'Go ahead, Vic,' said Hal. 'Show Roger that you can do it.'

Not very willingly, Vic went to the head of the slide. 'If an otter can do it, I can,' he said. He sat down and slid. He let out a yell of terror. He got up on his feet, intending to jump off the slide. Instead, he was thrown head first into the snowbank. He bored through it like a meteor and his head came out the other side while his feet dangled where he had entered.

'Get me out of here,' he screamed.

Just how do you get a man out of a snowbank? Vic's whole body, except head and feet, was buried. Hal and Temba laid hold of the head and tried to pull the screaming fellow out of his cage.

'Look out,' he cried. 'You're breaking my neck.'

It was not only snow that held him. It was also ice. The snowbank evidently had been there for a long time and every rain that fell upon it froze and became ice. In the grip of both snow and ice, Vic was helpless. However, that did not interfere with his yells and screams that sounded as if he were ready to give up the ghost at any moment.

'We'll have to chop him out,' said Hal. 'Get the axes.'

With ice-axes they began to attack the bank.

'Wait a minute,' cried Vic. 'You'll chop my head off.'

But the men kept chopping. They seemed to think it didn't matter very much if Vic lost his head. He didn't use it, so why should he mind losing it? But, after all, he was a human being, though a rather poor specimen, not as bright as an otter, so they kept on trying to release him in spite of the scolding they got for doing him this favour.

Vic was no longer scolding. He had fainted. The choppers finally got down to him and lifted out his unconscious body. He was almost as cold as ice. A Sherpa came with his sleeping bag.

'Put him in this. It will warm him up.'

It was a kind thing for the Sherpa to do and it was not his fault that Vic would have to scratch for a week because of the lice and fleas that had taken up residence in that bag.

The unconscious Vic was strapped to a sled and the company continued the struggle up the mountain.

Vic gradually came out of his faint and began scolding.

'Why am I in this lousy bag? I itch all over.' He squirmed and twisted, but he still itched. 'What are you doing to me? Don't you think I've had enough trouble? Let me out of this thing.'

They let him out of the sleeping bag. He was warm now. The hundreds of little biting things had warmed him up. But they had not improved his temper. He tottered along like a drunken man, grumbling at every step.

The higher they went, the thinner the air, and the thinner the air the less oxygen got to their lungs. The result was that they became dizzy, but Vic was the only one who complained about it.

At one point they faced a cliff thirty feet high. The Sherpas went a roundabout way to the top of the cliff and drove a sharp spike called a piton into the ice. They attached to this a rope ladder and let it down within reach of the others.

Hal climbed it without difficulty and so did Roger. Vic tried it, but the ladder wobbled so badly that he fell off.

'Why can't you hold it still?' he complained.

It was a foolish thing to say for there was no way the ladder could be held still. Made of rope, it swung and twisted at every step. The Hunts had climbed to the top of the masts on sailing ships. Vic had climbed nowhere except into bed. It was no use — he couldn't conquer the rope ladder.

'Hang on to it,' Hal called from above, 'and we'll haul you up.'

Vic sat down on a rung of the ladder and up he went like a heavy piece of baggage.

'You see,' he said, 'it's not so hard when you know how to do it.'

The weather grew worse as the day went on. They were now up in the clouds and the clouds were not kind. They struggled against a terrific wind. This was a blizzard, and it had no mercy. Breathing was almost impossible. Every head was aching, lungs were suffering for lack of air, eyes were attacked by pelting snow and rain that did not come down but flew horizontally in huge drops, making it seem that the horrible Yeti were determined to destroy them.

They lay flat on the ground and let the storm ride over them. No one spoke, because he could not be heard above the roar of the blizzard. Was it the Yeti who were trying to push them off the mountain?

If so, the Yeti did not succeed. They howled past and away and the clouds that enveloped the men broke and let a little sun come glimmering through.

Now they could speak and be heard, but all except the Sherpas were too exhausted to say anything. The Sherpas had been through all this sort of thing before. They lived high on the mountain and had become used to thin air and sudden storms.

It had not been possible to raise the two tents that had been brought along. The blizzard would have torn them to rags.

Now they painfully erected the tent for the three boys and the other tent for the Sherpas.

The boys crawled in, lit their oil stove, and cooked some dehydrated food — from which all the water had been squeezed out in order to make it lighter to carry.

Temba came in. He said, 'Do you want to go on up tomorrow morning, or will you go back to Aligar?'

'We'll go back,' said Vic.

Hal said to Vic, 'You can go back if you want to.

You will get lost and die on the way. We are not going back. Have you forgotten that we are after certain animals who live high up? As yet we haven't had a glimpse of a white tiger or a snow leopard or an ibex. That's what we came for, and we won't go back until we do our job.'

Vic protested, 'But how can I go on so long as I am covered by these pesky bugs that you let me get out of that Sherpa sleeping bag? I need a bath.'

Now they were up above the flowing streams and there was no water to be had. Hal said, 'You can use snow. There's plenty of that around. Take off your clothes, go outside and scrub yourself with snow.'

'But how about my clothes — they're full of bugs.'

'That's all right. We'll burn them.'

'Burn them? Then what will I wear?'

'We have some extra clothing. You can have it. The Sherpa who very kindly gave you his sleeping bag has taken it back, bugs and all. Your own sleeping bag is here ready for you whenever you need it. Try to be a good sport. Climbing the mountain should be great fun if you will just let yourself enjoy it.'

'Great fun!' Vic exclaimed. 'Buried in a snowbank, chopped out with ice-axes, climbing a rope ladder where there ought to be a flight of stairs. A howling blizzard full of Yeti. Bites all over me. Bathing in freezing cold snow. Great fun!'

'Cheer up,' said Hal. 'The worst is yet to come.'

27
The Deadly Avalanche

The boys remembered that their father wanted an ibex.

'What's an ibex?' Roger wanted to know. 'Is it something like the unicorn, an animal that doesn't really exist?'

'No,' said Hal. 'There's no such animal as a unicorn. But there really is an ibex. Right up here where there are so many rocks and precipices we are likely to find one. It's a sort of antelope with a dash of goat, a really remarkable animal. It has such keen eyesight that it can see you miles away. And it can smell you at the same distance. That's quite an improvement on poor little man who can smell only if he gets close up to something smellable.'

They had reached an altitude of seventeen thousand feet. The Sherpas did not mind this, but the boys, who never before had been above ten thousand, had headaches and were so dizzy that they could hardly see each other, let alone an ibex a mile or so away. They were gasping for air. They really got plenty of it but it was too thin to do them much good. They could have made use of oxygen bottles but they were too proud to give up.

'If the Sherpas can stand it, we can,' said Hal.

Temba came into the tent. 'Did you want an ibex? There's one on the rocks just above us.'

The boys at once forgot how they felt and rushed out to see the ibex. They were amazed by the two great horns of the beast, each five feet long.

'But how can it use them?' Roger wondered. 'They curve backwards. They can't kill another animal with horns that back up.'

'Right,' said Hal. 'But the ibex isn't interested in killing other animals. It lives on grass, plants, flowers, and the bark of trees.'

'Then it doesn't need horns at all,' said Roger. 'They are just a dead weight. Why do they grow them?'

'Let's say it's just one of Nature's mistakes. Or perhaps it's Nature's way of producing something beautiful. Those are very handsome horns.'

'They're handsome all right,' said Roger, 'but so far as I'm concerned I'd rather not be handsome than have such heavy horns. How much do you suppose they weigh?'

Hal thought a moment. 'I'd say the animal weighs about two hundred pounds, and a hundred of that is horns.'

'He doesn't seem to be afraid of us,' Vic said.

Hal said, 'Perhaps he doesn't know what dangerous creatures men are. Possibly he has never seen a man before.'

'Look at him leap,' Roger marvelled. 'I'll bet he jumped fifteen feet from one boulder to the next.

And that rock has only a point for him to stand on. See — he's clinging to it with all four feet. Why, he could walk a tightrope. I never saw any animal with such good balance.'

'Speaking of rope,' Hal said, 'I'd better try my lasso.'

It was a far throw, but Hal's fine muscles made light work of it. The loop settled down over the two magnificent horns. Since horns have no feeling the ibex was not aware that he had been caught. But when Hal began to draw in the rope, the ibex started dancing and prancing and pulling back with all his strength. But Hal drew him in to within ten feet and tied the rope to a piton whose sharp point was driven deep into the ice.

Hal spoke to Temba. 'Can you and your men strap him on to a sled and take him down to camp?'

'Yes,' said Temba, 'but not just now. Feel those quakes? They are very small but they generally mean that we're going to have a real earthquake in a few minutes. And that may cause an avalanche.'

'Avalanche?' Vic's voice trembled. He didn't know exactly what an avalanche was but it must be something bad.

Temba said, 'That's when everything comes tumbling down.'

The big shock came. The mountain trembled as if it had the ague. The snow was shaken off the upper slopes and came thundering down. Hal and Roger happened to be protected by a big rock. Vic was carried away.

There was snow below him, snow above him, snow packed firmly around him. He was suffocating for lack of air. He tried to get to the surface. He was swimming, moving arms and legs in a crawl. The surface must be very far away. The roar of flying rocks was terrific. Now and then rocks battered him or he ran into rocks that were not flying, and they knocked out of him what little breath he had.

He tried to inhale, but nothing came except snow. He continued to fight for air.

Now he was pinned under a block of ice. He remembered a story about someone who chiselled his way up through such a block of ice with his pocket knife. Vic had no knife, nor did he have enough strength left to do any chiselling.

Now he was out from under the block and swimming again but so weak that he could give up and die.

He had never thought that snow could make a noise, but now the snow was going boom, boom, boom, like a stampede of cattle. Half the time his heels were over his head and all the time he was spinning or rolling and the snow was exploding all about him. With the snow in his eyes he was blind, and so dazed that he thought he was already dead.

He was hanging over a precipice. He kept very quiet, because one movement might send him over the cliff. If he slipped and fell, what did it matter? Whether he died on top of the precipice or at the bottom, it was all the same.

The avalanche had come to a stop. Hal and Roger began to look for Vic. Below them there was nothing but snow, snow, and more snow. There was not one sign of human life down there. Temba and his men had survived, and they helped hunt for Vic.

Hal had something in his pocket that was called an 'electronic homing device'. It was designed for use after an avalanche to detect the presence of any person buried in the snow. Now was the time to make use of it.

He walked slowly down, holding the device. If there was anyone beneath him, the thing would go beep, beep, beep. It was hard going because the snow was not firm. It had been churned into powder by its rush down the mountain.

Roger went with him and also Temba and a Sherpa carrying a shovel. So far, there was nothing to shovel. They went a hundred feet down the slope, then another hundred, and another. The beeper was silent. After they had gone down a thousand feet they were about ready to give up. But Hal insisted upon continuing. On down to the fourteen-thousand-foot level. Here they stood on the edge of a precipice. There was a thousand-foot drop from the edge.

'I'm afraid he's not alive,' said Hal. 'If he went over that cliff and fell a thousand feet, he's dead.'

Just then the beeper began to beep.

'He's right here,' shouted Roger. Hal grabbed the shovel and began to dig. He was encouraged by the beeper which kept on playing its little tune.

At last the shovel poked something that wasn't snow. And it was too soft to be a rock. Feverishly, Hal dug around the soft thing until it was evident that this was Vic Stone in person, but perhaps Vic Stone dead.

His body was half over the edge of the precipice. His eyes were closed. His face was very pale, and badly scratched by rocks.

Hal took Vic's pulse. He could only faintly feel the beat of the pulse, but it was enough to tell him that Vic was alive.

They lifted his unconscious body out of the snow and, locking their hands beneath it, they carried it up three thousand feet to the place where the tents had been, and still were, though now they were flat on the ground.

The Sherpas had begun to erect them and soon it was possible to carry Vic inside and put him into his sleeping bag.

When he became warm he opened his eyes and seemed surprised to find that he was in a tent, not in heaven or hell. Hal was leaning over him with a cup of hot broth. The broth had to be spooned into Vic's mouth, for his arms were still numb.

'Who brought me here?' he asked.

Temba said, 'You owe your life to Hal and his little beeper. If it hadn't been for him you would still be under twenty feet of snow three thousand feet down the mountain. And you would be dead.'

Hal expected Vic to scold as usual. But Vic, with tears in his eyes, said, 'You're really a good guy.'

Hal was so astonished that he spilled the rest of the broth. The one who had tolerated the disaster better than anybody else was the ibex. He was quietened with the sleep-gun and two Sherpas took him on a sled down to Aligar.

The others went higher, still hoping to find those two unique animals, the snow leopard and the white tiger.

28
The Snow Leopard

'Today,' said Hal, 'we want to get a snow leopard. The best ones are in Tibet.'

Roger's eyes popped. 'Tibet! We must be hundreds of miles from Tibet.'

'Would you believe that Tibet is only two miles off?' Hal said.

'No, kind sir,' retorted Roger, 'I wouldn't believe it.'

'Well, it's true. There's a trail between these peaks to Tibet. We're not actually going into Tibet because we have no visa. But Temba tells me that some of the wild Tibetan animals wander over to the Indian side. So, that's where we'll look for them. Two that we especially want are the snow leopard and the yak.'

'There are plenty of yaks down in Aligar,' said Roger. 'There are yak pastures, full of yaks. The Sherpas use them to do all their farm work.'

'Right you are,' said Hal. 'But those yaks are small. The Tibetan yak is twice as big. That's the one we want. One of us will go after the yak and the other will go after the snow leopard.'

'Me for the snow leopard,' said Roger.

'But that's the dangerous one,' Hal warned.

'I know,' said Roger. 'I'll take one of your tear-gas pistols. And a sleep-gun. And a sled with a couple of our Sherpas to pull it — in case we find a snow leopard and put it to sleep, they can take it down to Aligar.'

Hal did not like the idea of his brother tackling any leopard, the most ferocious of all cats.

'Very well, since you are determined, you bring home a snow leopard and I'll try to produce a big yak.'

'Where do I come in?' said Vic.

Hal stared. It was the first time Vic had ever offered to do anything.

'Vic,' Hal said, 'I'd like to have you go down to Aligar and see if the blue bear and the ibex are being properly cared for. They are extremely valuable animals and we don't want to take any chances of neglect or injury. The mayor is supposed to be taking care of them.'

So the three boys started out, each in a different direction. First we shall follow the fortunes of Roger, in search of a snow leopard.

Followed by his two Sherpas with their sled he trudged off close to the line between India and Tibet. They were at an altitude of twenty thousand feet and the air was so thin that Roger often had to stop to breathe. He had forgotten to bring along an oxygen bottle. The Sherpas did not mind the altitude for they had grown up on the mountain.

There was no sun this morning and the wind was ice cold. His feet, hands and ears were the first parts of him to turn numb with frostbite. He was becoming 'altitude-sick'. He staggered, and fell down in the snow. He refused to let the Sherpas help him and struggled to his feet and walked on. The mountainside was very steep here and it would be easy to fall. In that case you would keep on falling for thousands of feet and probably wind up dead.

It would be safer if they were roped together. A Sherpa produced a rope and tied it first to Roger, then, at a distance of six feet, to the other Sherpa, and finally, after another six feet, to himself.

Now, if Roger began to fall, there were two strong men to hold him back. The Sherpas had no idea that they would be the ones to fall. They had so much confidence in their own ability that they did not wear crampon spikes on the soles of their boots. Roger was not so cocksure. He not only wore crampons, but he carried an ice-axe and frequently plunged the point of it into the ice in order to keep himself from slipping.

All of a sudden he heard a yell behind him and the two Sherpas shot downhill like rockets.

Roger stabbed the point of his ice-axe into the ice, but the weight of two falling bodies on the rope tied about his waist nearly yanked him loose in spite of crampons and axe.

So he saved the Sherpas from what might have been a fatal fall of thousands of feet. They clambered back to his level and from that moment regarded him with more respect. He was just a boy, but a tough one.

Roger had only a moment to think how smart he

was. The jolt he had suffered had shaken off his snow-glasses. Then he had accidentally stepped on them and broken them to bits. To complete his misery the sun, which had been hiding behind clouds, suddenly burst out in its full glory and fury. The glare of sunlight on snow and ice was too much for his eyes. He blacked out. For a time he sat in the snow.

When he dared to open his eyes he saw double, even triple. His feet, when he looked at them, were a mile away. His mind played him tricks. He was in the Gir Forest capturing a golden langur. No, he was in a Tibetan monastery looking at Yeti relics. He could see only dimly. Although the sun was blazing, it seemed to him that everything was a dark grey.

The Sherpas knew what to do in a case of snow blindness. They would cover their eyes with their own hair so that they could just see out between hairs, and most of the glare, terrific at these altitudes, was cut off. Roger's hair was not very long, but they managed to get a few wisps of it over his eyes and at once he felt a great relief.

Frostbite played a peculiar game. At first his toes and fingers tingled painfully. Then the pain gradually disappeared and he thought he had beaten the frostbite.

The fact was that the frostbite had beaten him and had made his feet and hands and nose so numb that he no longer felt the least pain. When he got up and tried to walk it seemed as if his feet had been amputated and replaced by wooden pegs.

The Sherpas were making a peculiar call. It
sounded exactly like the voice of a leopard. If a
snow leopard were anywhere near by, it would
answer that call and come close.

It was a good plan and it worked. There came
an answering call from behind a great rock. Then
the animal leaped to the top of the rock.

What a sight he was. Not at all like the leopards
of the Gir Forest. He was snow white except for a
few black rings here and there. His whiskers and
moustache and chest were perfectly white. He was
about five feet long without a tail, and the tail
was another five feet long. It looked more like a
python than a tail. It was as thick through as that
serpent and was the same width all the way to the

end. It must have been pretty heavy to carry around, but it was beautiful.

The animal's belly was pure white, without rings. The fur was long, thick and soft, a lovely warm overcoat against the chill air of twenty thousand feet.

The great tail was switching back and forth angrily. He had heard the call of a mate and now he had found no mate, only these impertinent humans. He tensed himself for a spring. But he did not spring because at that instant Roger used his tear-gas pistol. This was enough to stop anything alive, either beast or human. The leopard blasted the air with his roar, blinked, and shook his great head. He leaped from the rock towards his tormentors. But at the same moment Roger fired his sleep-gun and the dart penetrated the snow-white patch between rings on the animal's flank. The boy and the Sherpas jumped out of the way and the leopard found nothing but snow and ice when he landed. He was still full of fire and made for the boy who should be the easiest one to kill. Roger stopped him with another shot of tear gas. The big cat collapsed within two feet of his intended victim.

One of the Sherpas, thinking that the cat was now asleep, put his foot on the furry body. That nearly cost him his life. The animal turned on him and would have torn him to ribbons if Roger had not fired another dart, and both the tear gas and the sleep medicine conquered one of the finest trophies that the Hunts had ever collected.

After they were very sure that the dangerous animal was sound asleep it took all three of them to lift his two-hundred-pound body on to the sled. Then they started back to camp. A little later the sleeping cat would be taken to Aligar.

In the meantime, Hal had found his yak. Of all shaggy animals, this was the shaggiest. Its hair hung down so low that it brushed the ground. The animal stood six feet high and Hal estimated its weight at twelve hundred pounds. Its two long horns looked dangerous but the animal was not a fighter and the horns were merely ornaments, not weapons.

Its feet were hidden by the long waterfall of fur. It was all dark brown except for a white muzzle.

It didn't seem to mind Hal's close inspection. Hal lifted part of the shaggy coat and discovered that beneath it there was a thick undercoat of warm woolly hair. This, he knew, was plaited into rope by the Tibetans so that a team of yaks would be harnessed by their own hair.

This animal, however, had never been in a team and was completely wild. It had never been taught to fear man. Its eyesight and hearing were not so good but it had a keen sense of smell. Apparently it had no objection to the smell of this human and so long as it was gently treated the noose that Hal had put over its horns was willingly accepted. Hal led it back to camp. As soon as was convenient it would be taken down to Aligar. Certainly it was a unique wild animal, rarely seen in any zoo.

Vic, who had been sent down to see if the animals were being properly cared for, reached Aligar with-

out getting lost. He looked at the great blue bear in its cage, and the fine ibex in another.

He had followed Hal and Roger to the mountains with the intention of stealing their animals. Now he had his opportunity. With the help of some men he could get the two cages up on to the truck and drive away.

Somehow he had lost his taste for such an adventure. Hal had trusted him, and Vic couldn't do anything so mean as steal his animals. Besides, Hal had saved him from certain death. He was grateful.

This was a new feeling for Vic. He was not used to being grateful for anything. He had always taken great pleasure in being a skunk. He couldn't understand why he felt differently now.

After chatting with the mayor and making sure that the animals were being properly fed, he made

**the long trek back to the camp at twenty thousand
feet.**

29
The White Tiger

Tiger! Tiger! burning bright
In the forest of the night,
What immortal hand or eye
Could frame thy fearful symmetry?

The boys had one big job left to do. To get a tiger. Not just any tiger. They already had two of the usual sort, with yellow hide and black stripes.

These were valuable animals, but the most valuable was yet to be captured. It was the remarkable white tiger.

There were said to be some on the white slopes of the Himalayas. Since John Hunt had asked for one, the boys could not go home without capturing a white tiger.

Roger had brought in a snow leopard. Hal was not feeling well.

'Then it's up to me,' said Vic.

'But you can't do it alone,' said Hal.

Vic said, 'I can try.'

Hal and Roger could hardly believe their ears. It

was unusual for Vic to try to do anything, except to steal animals.

'Go ahead and try,' said Hal. 'Don't be discouraged if you fail. There are very few white tigers — we haven't seen one yet.'

Vic set out to find a white tiger. All day he searched, with no result. Another day, and another and another he hunted in vain. He kept at it. Hal had given him his life — he must give Hal a white tiger.

One day, passing a rock cave, he heard a curious snuffling sound inside.

He stopped and looked in. At first he could see nothing because his eyes were half blinded by sun and snow. But his ears did better than his eyes. A tremendous roar seemed to shake the cave.

Vic retreated. If only he could find a tree or bush to hide behind. But there was nothing of the sort at this altitude. So he simply stood still.

Gradually his eyes became adjusted to the darkness and he saw what he had been looking for. It was a white tiger of tremendous size. He had heard that the world's biggest tiger was the Siberian, fourteen feet long. This must be the next biggest. What a trophy, if he could get it.

The hide of this remarkable animal was white with a few black stripes, not yellow and black like most tigers.

As his vision improved he could make out five little blobs around the monster's feet. They were white tiger cubs, and this must be their mother.

She would fiercely defend her cubs even if it meant her own death.

It would have been prudent for Vic to walk away. But he was not prudent when he saw the chance of getting this great tigress and her cubs. The cubs were really as important as the mother. There were probably both males and females among these youngsters, and there was a good chance that on John Hunt's wild-animal farm the line of white tigers could be continued down the years. Therefore every one of these five was precious.

Tigers seldom attack unless disturbed. As long as Vic stood still the tigress did not move.

There was a growl behind him and he wanted to run but mastered his fear and remained quiet. Another tiger passed him and entered the cave. This must be the father of the cubs. But it did something that no good father would do. In spite of the protesting growl of the tigress, the father picked up one of the cubs and ate it.

Hal had mentioned that this sort of thing could happen. Tiger fathers frequently eat their own young. They seem to forget that they are fathers, but the mother never forgets that she is the mother. The tiger seemed ready to continue his meal by devouring another cub.

Vic could not let this happen. He let fly a jet of tear gas into the face of the tiger who immediately gave up the idea of completing his dinner and ran out of the cave.

The tigress looked at Vic with apparent gratitude, and if she had been able to speak she doubtless would have said, 'Thank you.'

For the first time Vic noticed that the tigress was standing on three feet and holding up the other paw as if it were too painful to set it on the ground. Was there a thorn in that paw, or the quill of a porcupine?

Vic very, very slowly walked into the cave, stopping every once in a while to let the tigress get used to his presence. He went to the side of the tigress away from the cubs and stood there for a while looking at that lifted paw.

The tigress rumbled a bit, but did not growl. Anyone who had saved her cubs could not be all bad.

Vic squatted down so that he could see the wounded paw. There was no thorn in it and no quill. But there was an arrowhead deeply embedded in the flesh. No one on the Indian side of the mountain used arrows, therefore it must have been fired by a Tibetan.

Very gently, Vic lifted the foot and drew out the arrowhead. The tigress turned to look at him and again he thought he saw gratitude in her eyes. She even spoke. She said, 'Ouf,' and followed that with 'Aum.' Vic was not up on tiger language, but accepted these remarks as being friendly.

She now took to washing her four cubs just as a house cat washes her kittens.

Now Vic dared to do something very dangerous. He picked up the four tiny cubs, put two in one pocket and two in another. The tigress grumbled and worried but could not attack such a friend. Vic walked very slowly out of the cave and the tigress followed, and kept on following until they arrived at the camp.

Sherpas who had been standing about saw the monster approach. They rushed into their tent and closed it firmly against this great killer. Hal and Roger came out and Vic told them the whole story. Then the tigress was put to sleep and she, along with a bagful of her precious babies, was sledded down to Aligar.

Hal put an arm around Vic and said, 'From now on you're our brother.'

'That's what I'd like to be,' said Vic.

Later on, Hal slipped a cheque for $250 into Vic's pocket for the capture of five remarkable animals.

30
The Yeti Mystery

Their animal collection complete, the boys and the Sherpas returned to Aligar.

They had one more job to do. John Hunt had asked them to investigate what the world called the Abominable Snowman and the people of the mountains called the Yeti.

'The main thing for us to find out,' said Hal, 'is whether there are Yeti or not. Are they real, or just imaginary? Most of the mountain people believe they are real. In Katmandu they believe it. In Bhutan, shut in by the Himalayas, they have great stories about these unseen creatures. The Yeti are called "the national animals of Bhutan". They even put a picture of the Yeti on their postage stamps.'

'If everybody believes it, it must be true,' said Roger.

'Not quite,' said Hal. 'There was a time when everyone believed the earth was flat. They were all wrong. Even in these countries there are some who don't believe in Yeti. I think that shopkeeper is one of them. The head lama is perhaps another. The relics they tried to sell us may not be real Yeti scalps, or Yeti arms, or Yeti tails, or have anything at all to do with Yeti. I don't know. We'll just have to find out. First let's go to see that shopkeeper who tried to sell us what he called a Yeti scalp.'

They dropped in at the store and were enthusiastically received.

'Ah,' said the shopkeeper, 'you came to buy that Yeti scalp.'

'Well,' said Hal, 'we've been thinking about it. But first I'd like to have you come down to the mayor's garden where our animals are stored. I think you'll be interested to see them. Bring along the Yeti scalp.'

The man called his wife to take care of the shop and went with the boys to see the magnificent white tiger and the cubs, the beautiful snow leopard, the ibex, the Tibetan yak and finally the blue bear. The shopkeeper was much pleased and impressed.

'And now you have come back to buy the Yeti scalp,' he said.

'Let me have it for a moment,' said Hal.

The blue bear was lying at the side of his cage and some of his hair projected between the wires. Hal placed the furry scalp beside the fur of the blue bear.

'Do you notice anything?' he asked the shopkeeper.

'Can't say I do,' replied the shopkeeper.

'You don't notice that the hair on the scalp and the hair on the blue bear are exactly the same?'

'Well, now that you speak of it, there is a slight similarity.'

'Not just a slight similarity,' said Hal, 'they are exactly the same. In other words, that scalp was made from the skin of a blue bear, not a Yeti. And you tried to sell it to us for a lot of money.'

The shopkeeper was full of excuses. 'How did I know the scalp was made of blue bear skin? The man who sold it to me said it was a true Yeti scalp. I took his word for it. I can't help it if he was not honest and reliable.'

Hal felt like saying that he couldn't help it if the shopkeeper was not honest and reliable. Instead, he merely smiled and returned the scalp to the shopkeeper.

'Please sir,' said that gentleman, 'don't tell anybody about this.' He walked back to the shop with his fake Yeti scalp.

The boys went in to thank the mayor for taking good care of the animals. Hal paid him more rupees than he had ever seen at one time in his life.

'Glad to be of service,' said the mayor. 'That's what we are here for. We also like to provide our guests with some of these Yeti relics.' And he laid them out on the floor.

The two young naturalists examined them very carefully. One that the mayor said was the arm of a Yeti was really the hind leg of a Himalayan bear. A 'Yeti claw' had really come from a black bear. A beautiful white rug said to be the skin of a Yeti was a skin all right, but the skin of a snow leopard.

The two investigators left to meet their friend the head lama, and Hal asked, 'When you saw the Yeti through the window, did you take a photograph of him?'

'No,' said the lama, 'he was gone before I could get my camera out.'

'Have you ever seen a photograph of a Yeti?'

'I can't say that I have. But in the magazine called *Yeti*, published in Katmandu, I read about a yogi who had taken a picture of a Yeti. People came to his home to see it but they never could get him to show them the picture. He always sent them word that he was meditating and could not be disturbed.'

'But I don't understand,' said Hal, 'why the picture he had taken was not reproduced with the article in the magazine. What did he say in that article?'

'He claimed that he had encountered the Yeti on a glorious day with snowflakes flying in the air. By the way, I have the article. You can read it for yourself. It is in English.'

Hal and Roger read the article by the yogi whose name was Nath. The yogi wrote:

All was still and calm. I was chanting Hindu prayers when I suddenly saw the greatest spectacle of my life. I knew it was the Yeti, the great Snowman, the thing we have been taking about for years. I was astonished. As he drew closer he looked in my direction. He nodded his head and continued hopping or limping as he moved. Then the Yeti went away and disappeared into the misty clouds that hang over the mountain. Before he left I got his picture. When he was gone my companions caught up with me and were surprised to find me in a dazed condition. I pointed in the direction of the disappearing

Yeti, but my friends said they could see nothing. The creature was seven arms tall, and as stout as a barrel. He had long arms and a short neck, a pointed head, and was hairy all over. He had no tail. The footprints he left were enormous.

But the picture the yogi said he had taken was not published with the article and was never seen by anyone.

Hal suspected that the whole thing had been dreamed up by the yogi during his meditations.

The lama also had relics that he was willing to sell at high prices. The yogi had said his Yeti had no tail. The lama insisted the Yeti he had met did have a tail, and here it was. He laid it down on the floor. Hal took it up and examined it. He recognized it as the tail of a golden langur.

The lama had other relics, all supposed to be parts of Yeti — scalps, teeth, jawbones, claws, arms and legs.

He said he had a complete Yeti hide. He didn't want to sell it, but would show it for a thousand rupees.

Hal guessed that the reason he didn't want to sell it was because if he kept it he could show it over and over and over again at a thousand rupees a time.

'How is it that we see no skulls of Yeti?' Hal asked.

'There are not many of them,' said the lama. 'I have the two best ones.'

He brought them out. Hal at once identified them. One was the skull of a dog. The other was the skull of a gorilla.

The next thing that was laid before them was an immense tooth. The lama informed them that a Yeti with toothache had torn the tooth from its mouth and thrown it in the snow. It could be bought for two hundred dollars.

'All very interesting,' said Hal. He did not say that this was the tooth of a Himalayan bear. 'I'd like to buy it but it will take nearly all the money we have to ship our animals to New York. We have enough to pay for our lodging here if you will allow us to sleep on the floor for a few nights.'

'You are more than welcome,' said the lama. He swept up his 'true Yeti relics' and stored them away. He said he must go and meditate, and he left the room.

Perhaps he meditated on how to convince these boys that Yeti were real, not just creatures of imagination.

The boys walked through the village. They looked again at the great five-foot print outside the shopkeeper's door. They remembered large footprints they had seen elsewhere in their climb up and down the mountain. The people had said these were made by enormous Yeti.

'How about that?' Roger asked. 'Those huge footprints?'

'That isn't very mysterious,' Hal said. 'If you make a print in the snow with your boot and come back a couple of days later and look at it you will imagine that it would have been made by a monster.'

'But how does it get so big?'

'The sun. A couple of days of strong sun and the

edges of your footprint will be melted so that it looks like the footprint of a giant. Try it and see.'

Roger did try it and found it was so. The sun had so enlarged the footprint that the superstitious folk on the mountain might easily suppose it to have been made by a giant Yeti.

The boys could report to their father that there was no scientific proof of the existence of Yeti even though most of the inhabitants of the Himalayas believed in them.

31
Mountains Make Men

In the small telegraph and telephone office Hal phoned New Delhi for five trucks to transport his animals to Bombay and load them on the freighter *Horizon* for New York. He cabled his father as follows:

LET ME KNOW IF YOU HAVE RECEIVED OUR FIRST SHIPMENT OF ANIMALS. A SECOND SHIPMENT WILL COME TO YOU ON THE FREIGHTER 'HORIZON' CARRYING A BLUE BEAR, IBEX, YAK, SNOW LEOPARD CAUGHT BY ROGER, ALSO A WHITE TIGER AND FOUR WHITE TIGER CUBS CAPTURED BY VIC STONE.

Two days later he received his father's answer:

YOU AMAZE ME. WE RECEIVED YOUR FIRST SHIPMENT OF ANIMALS AND NOW YOU ARE SENDING MORE. I ASKED FOR SIXTEEN ANIMALS AND YOU ARE GIVING ME TWENTY-FIVE. YOUR VIC STONE MUST BE QUITE A MAN — CAPTURING NOT ONLY THE FABULOUS WHITE TIGER, BUT FOUR WHITE TIGER CUBS WHO WILL KEEP THE WHITE

TIGER FAMILY GROWING IN ZOOS THAT HAVE NEVER SEEN A WHITE TIGER. GOOD WORK. CONGRATULATIONS TO YOU, ROGER AND STONE. BETTER COME HOME NOW AND GET BACK TO SCHOOL AND COLLEGE.

Hal said to Roger, 'Dad is right about Vic. The mountains made a man of him. He had a lot of tough experiences and they toughened him. All the hard climbing, tackling a rope ladder, nearly frozen in a howling blizzard, covered with bites after using a Sherpa sleeping bag full of lice and fleas, forced to take a bath in snow, and worst of all, buried in an avalanche where he could hardly breathe and felt his last day had come, then performing that difficult and dangerous job of capturing a white tiger and cubs — it all changed him from a thieving nincompoop into a real man.'

'Of course there's one more thing that changed him,' said Roger. 'You dug him up. He never appreciated you before. Now he would do anything in the world for you.'

They didn't dream that within half an hour Vic was going to do just that for Hal.'

'While we're waiting for the trucks,' Hal said, 'let's go out and take a look at a glacier. There's a big one just outside the village.'

They found Vic and the three of them explored the glacier. It was a great sheet of ice inching slowly down the mountain. Roger had always thought of a glacier as being perfectly smooth and was astonished to find that this one was full of giant cracks called crevasses that made walking extremely

231

dangerous. Some of the crevasses were a hundred feet deep. They came to one that was partly bridged over by snow and ice.

'Do we dare cross it?' Roger wondered. 'Perhaps it will break under our weight.'

'I'll try it,' Hal said.

He stepped on it. 'I think it's solid,' he said. Very cautiously he walked out to the middle of the bridge.

Then there was a crackling sound, the snow bridge gave way, and Hal dropped a hundred feet to the bottom of the great crack.

Fortunately the rocks at the bottom were covered with snow — but the snow had hardened and Hal landed with a jolt that knocked the breath out of him and made his mind a blank. He lay there as if dead, his eyes closed, and with no movement of his arms or legs. Roger and Vic called to him but got no answer. He was unconscious. A hundred-foot fall was enough to kill even a man as strong as Hal.

'A rope!' exclaimed Vic. 'We've got to have a rope.' He set out at a run for the village. He came back in a few minutes with a rope and some Sherpas.

If Hal could take hold of the rope and hang on, they could pull him up. They lowered the rope until the end of it lay on his body. They shouted, hoping to wake him up. He was far gone. He did not stir.

'I'll go down,' said Vic. 'I'll tie the rope around him and you can hoist him up.'

'You can't do that,' said Roger, but he was speaking to the old Vic, not the new one. Vic went down the rope hand over hand and landed beside Hal's body. He put his fingers on his friend's wrist. He could feel a very faint heartbeat. 'He's alive!' he shouted to those above. He put the rope around the body, just below the armpits. He tied it fast.

'Haul away,' he shouted.

Roger and the Sherpas drew the body slowly up between the two ice walls of the crevasse and finally Hal, still unconscious, lay on the snow well away from the great crack that had swallowed him.

For the time being Vic was forgotten. Roger did what he could to revive his brother and the Sherpas had their own ideas of first aid. At last, Hal opened his eyes.

'What's been going on?' he said.

'You've been giving us a big scare,' said Roger. 'We were afraid you were dead.'

'What nonsense,' said Hal. 'Why did you think I was dead?'

'Don't you remember? You fell into the crevasse.'

'I did no such thing,' said Hal indignantly.

'You tried to cross the bridge. It broke and you fell.'

'Then how did I get here?'

'Vic went down and roped you and the men pulled you up.'

Hal looked around. 'Where's Vic?'

Everyone had forgotten about Vic. They looked over the edge. There he was, deep down, lying on the snow, recovering from the unusual exertion of climbing down a hundred feet of rope.

They once more let down the rope and Vic tried to tie himself into it. It was a lot of trouble, because in this great icy refrigerator his hands were numb with cold.

He was hauled up the ice wall to the top and was glad to see Hal actually on his feet as if nothing had happened. Vic extended a frost-bitten hand and Hal took it.

Vic said, 'I'm so glad to see you're still alive and kicking.'

'If you hadn't come after me,' said Hal, 'by this time I'd be as dead as an icicle.'

The next day the trucks came and the animals of the high Himalayas began their trip to the wild-animal farm of John Hunt and Sons.

32
What's a Father For?

Vic was taken to the hospital on the plains below.

It was not just his rescue of Hal that had exhausted him, but the strain of capturing a great white tiger, and especially his near-death experience buried alive in the avalanche.

'You have pulmonary embolism,' the doctor told him, 'and a bad case of edema.'

'What's that?' queried Vic.

'Water on the lungs. It makes it difficult for oxygen to reach your arteries.'

Hal had gone with him to see him safely bedded down in the hospital. Now Hal cabled Vic's father, Robert Stone, in Cleveland.

YOUR SON IS DANGEROUSLY ILL. HE IS IN THE HOSPITAL AT NEW DELHI. HE IS NOT THE VIC YOU KNEW. NOW HE HAS BECOME A MAN WORTHY OF YOUR LOVE. HE HAS SAVED MY LIFE. YOU CAN SAVE HIM.

Two days later Vic looked up to see his father standing beside his bed. Vic had been thinking about dying. Now he began to think about living.

'Dad,' he said, 'you made that long trip just to see me. I thought you had given me up as a bad job. Now I know I'm going to get better.'

'Of course you will,' said Robert Stone. 'And I'll stay until you do. Then you are going home with me. I've been lonesome without you.'

Under the care of a British doctor and encouraged by his father, Vic rapidly recovered. He and his father went back to Parkwood Drive, Cleveland, Ohio.

Vic, who had always been a braggart, never bragged about his adventures in the Himalayas. He did brag about Hal Hunt. 'He and his brother — great guys,' he said.

He was a great guy himself. His father thought, 'Vic — short for Victory. Victory over himself.'

Hal and Roger went home to a warm reception from parents and friends. They saw again the fine animals they had taken *alive* — a job far more difficult than shooting them *dead*.

Back to the schoolbooks. But it was most curious how the algebra and geometry kept fading from the page to be replaced by a misty vision of the Gir Forest and the high Himalayas.

Other Adventure Books

The reader is also invited to read **Amazon Adventure**, an account of the experiences of Hal and Roger on an expedition to collect wild animals in the Amazon jungle; **South Sea Adventure**, a story of pearls, a desert island and a raft; **Underwater Adventure**, on the thrills of skin diving in the tropical seas; **Volcano Adventure**, a story of descent into the mountains of fire; **Whale Adventure**, about the monster that sank a ship; **African Adventure**, an exciting tale of the land of big game; **Elephant Adventure**, on a hazardous hunt in the Mountains of the Moon; **Safari Adventure**, on the war against poachers; **Lion Adventure**, on the capture of a man-eater; **Gorilla Adventure**, on the life of a great ape; **Diving Adventure**, set in a city beneath the sea; **Cannibal Adventure**, set in the perilous jungles of New Guinea; and **Arctic Adventure**, set in the snowbound wastes of the polar regions.